Stinky Finky

Valerie H. Wilson

ISBN:1494915022
ISBN-13: 9781494915025

DEDICATION

To my husband, Bill, who encouraged me to share my characters in a book and was my first editor.

CONTENTS

ACKNOWLEDGMENTS

Thanks to Mary Clark for convincing me to publish, providing technical help, and editing my book.

Thanks, too, to Julie Taylor, who shared this story with her students and edited the novel word by word.

More thanks to Mrs. Taylor's students whose enthusiastic response to this novel convinced me to share it with the public.

And special thanks to my family whose love and support made this novel possible.

CHAPTER 1: FAST FACT FAILURES

"No recess!" Molly could not believe what she was hearing. Her teacher, Miss Bees, must have made a mistake. Molly had never missed a recess in all the years she had been in school. She never did anything really bad and she always turned in her homework. Why would Miss Bees take away her recess? Molly put her head down on her desk and covered her face with her arms. She didn't want anyone in her class to see that she had tears in her eyes. She had been looking forward to recess all morning. It was a beautiful spring day and after the long New England winter, it would have been great to play outdoors. Plus her best friend, Addy, had brought her new doll and its new clothes to play with during their playtime. Peaking under her left arm, she saw that Addy was whispering to the girls around her. Molly knew they were talking about her. She hid her face in her arms again.

"You three stay in the room," yelled Miss Bees. "I'll be right back to talk to you once I take the class outside to meet the recess aide."

Molly wondered who the other two kids were that had to miss recess. She waited until she heard the door close before she lifted up her head. She needed to get the tears off of her face without the other two seeing her. She casually raised her hand pretending to fix her curly black hair. Quickly she wiped away the tears and turned to see who was left in the room behind her.

"Oh, no!" she thought. It was bad enough that she had to miss recess, but look who the other two students were. Sitting in a desk two rows back and to the left was the skinny girl, Sue. Molly didn't think she had ever heard the girl say one thing in the five years they had been going to school together. "Skinny and wimpy," Molly thought. Sue was not only quiet; she had stringy, ugly hair and horrible clothes. Well, not that many clothes. Molly thought that Sue only had four or five things she wore to school. And they were all ugly. They were all dresses. Who wore dresses all the time? And the dresses had funny sewing on the front. They were pretty much faded out too.

None of Sue's clothing looked like the outfits that Molly wore.

Molly had wonderful clothing. She wished she could say that she went to the store and picked them out herself, but she couldn't. Being only ten, she really couldn't go to stores alone. Besides, her mother wouldn't let her pick out her own outfits anyway. Her mother, Molly thought, liked everything to match. Molly's shirt matched her pants. Her socks matched one of the colors in her shirt. Her shoes matched the socks. Even her hair barrettes or scrunchies matched her rest of her outfit.

Pretending to adjust her shirt, Molly turned to see who the third prisoner from recess was. She peeked to the right behind her. "Could this get any worse," Molly thought. Sitting at his desk and looking right at her was the new kid, Juan. Juan had joined their class a few weeks ago. He probably wouldn't miss today's recess because he never played with anyone outside anyway. He didn't even speak English. Molly didn't know where he was from, but she thought maybe it was Mexico or some island. He sometimes answered Miss Bees' questions with the word, "Si." Molly had heard that on her Saturday morning shows. But Juan didn't look anything like the characters from those cartoons. All of the people who spoke Spanish on TV had dark hair and dark eyes. This Juan kid was short like Molly. He had light brown hair and blue eyes.

However, he always dressed in dark clothing. Molly thought that he only owned one set of school clothes. He always wore a black t-shirt and black jeans. Even his sneakers were black.

This was the worst day in Molly's life. Not only did she have to miss recess, she was being kept inside with the two poor kids in her class. Maybe Miss Bees had made a terrible mistake and kept Molly in because she thought Molly was a poor kid who needed free lunch.

Just then, the door opened and Miss Bees walked in. Molly didn't much like Miss Bees. She thought that her teacher was kind of scary looking. Miss Bees was very tall and very thin, like a scarecrow. Her gray hair was cut in a very short, unattractive style. Molly also didn't think that Miss Bees was a good teacher. That lady never really explained anything. She would stand in the front of the room for a few minutes and mumble. Then she would pass out worksheets and tell the class to work quietly. She never walked around the room when Molly and her classmates were working on the sheets. Instead, Miss Bees would go back and sit at her desk. Molly sometimes wondered what she was doing there. When the kids would finish with their worksheets, they would bring them to the counter and carefully sort them into the right basket. There was a basket for reading, one for spelling, one for social studies, one for science, and one for math. Molly didn't mind putting the worksheets in the right basket. She had plenty of practice with that kind of organization at home. Her mother loved filing things in the correct container.

Molly's thoughts about her mother were interrupted by Miss Bees' loud voice.

"I hate to have to keep you three inside on such a nice day, but you know that you haven't met the goal for this month in math."

Molly had no idea what that old witch Miss Bees was talking about. What goal in math? She had turned in all her math homework and all her math worksheets. She knew she had put them in the right baskets every day.

"Ah, Miss Bees," Molly said. "I think there has been a big mistake. I've done all my work in math. So I'll just go and get my jacket and go outside." She started to stand up from her desk.

"Not so fast, young lady," Miss Bees yelled at her. "You have NOT met the goal for this month in math. I told the whole class that everyone, and I mean everyone, will get all 30 facts right on the fast fact test by the end of the month. You three are ruining my record! Everyone in my class always gets all 30 facts right on the fast fact test by this time of the year."

Molly was stunned. She didn't even know what the old biddy was talking about. Just then, Molly heard a faint whispering.

"Excuse me, Miss Bees."

Who was talking? Molly spun around in her seat. She couldn't believe her ears or her eyes. It was that Sue girl. She was talking and she was talking to the teacher.

"Excuse me, Miss Bees. But I don't think you can expect Juan to get all the facts right on the fast fact test. He just got here and they probably don't teach multiplication wherever he came from. Couldn't he be excused?"

"What?" bellowed Miss Bees. "No one gets exempted from the fast fact test."

Slowly, the situation was becoming clearer to Molly. She was being forced to stay inside because of some stupid game that Miss Bees liked to play with the class. The fast facts activity was one of the few times during the day that Miss Bees would actually get up from sitting at her desk. Miss Bees would go to the front of each row and count out one worksheet for each of the people in the row. She would pass them out face down. Then she would announce loudly, as Miss Bees never seemed to talk in the normal voice, that no one should look at the paper until she gave the signal. After everyone had a paper, Miss Bees would hold up her stopwatch and roar, "On your mark, get set, go!" After flipping the paper over, the kids would have one minute to write down the answer to each of the 30 multiplication facts on the page. At the end of 60 seconds, Miss Bees would yell, "Stop!" The hand that was holding the pencil had to be raised in the air. You couldn't even finish writing your last answer.

Molly had never worried much about what she was doing on the fast fact test. Sometimes she peeked over to see what numbers that smart girl, Ellie, was writing and copied them. When Miss Bees passed them back there was never a grade on the paper. No big red A or 100. Not even a sticker if you got them all right. Everyone knew that if there wasn't a grade on the paper, it didn't count for your report card and if it didn't count for your report card, it just couldn't be that important. Her friend Addy got them all right the first time the class had done the fast facts and she didn't even get extra free time.

Besides, Molly couldn't figure out why she needed to know the multiplication facts anyway. She wasn't really sure what multiplication was. Plus, she had a calculator. For the few times that Miss Bees gave them math homework, Molly got out that calculator and tapped away at the numbers. Math homework never took long.

"Miss Plies, Miss Plies would you please pay attention to me?"

Molly's face reddened as she looked up at Miss Bees who was standing right in front of her desk. "Now I can understand why you don't know your facts when you won't even pay attention to me when I am trying to give you extra help during recess."

"Sorry, Miss Bees," Molly mumbled.

Miss Bees continued. "Everyone else in fourth grade has already mastered the fast fact test. Until you three can get all 30 facts correct in one minute, you will have to continue to stay in at recess and memorize the multiplication table. Do you all understand me?"

Molly nodded her head and glanced back at the other two. Sue was nodding her head, but she looked a little bit angry. The new kid, Juan, was also nodding his head.

Molly didn't know what she was going to do. She knew that she wouldn't learn all the multiplication facts by the next day. She didn't even know how you learned the multiplication facts. She also knew that she wouldn't get any help at home. She couldn't ask her father to help her because he got home from work late. Her mother told her not to bother her father when he got home because he needed time to unwind. Molly wasn't quite sure what that meant, but she stayed away from her father. Her mother couldn't help her, especially now. Molly's mother was the chairwoman of the school carnival this year. The fair was only a couple of weeks away so she was extra busy. Molly's mother was the chairwoman of something every year. Everyone always marveled at how organized Molly's mother was and how well she ran things.

Molly worried that she would never have recess again. She looked back at Sue. Sue still looked angry. Before Miss Bees could yell at them anymore, the door opened and her classmates came back in from recess. Molly looked for her friend Addy. When Addy came in she was giggling with Sarah and Shannon. Molly knew that she had lost her best

friend just because of Miss Bees and her stupid fast facts.

CHAPTER 2: SURPRISES FROM SUE

Most afternoons, Molly rode home on the bus. She always sat with Addy. Today she had to meet her mother in the cafeteria after school. Molly was glad. She didn't want to have to sit on the bus by herself while Addy sat with Sarah and Shannon. Molly's mother was going to have a meeting of the other mothers who were helping with the school carnival this year.

The school carnival was one of the big events of the year in their small Massachusetts town. Although they were close enough to drive easily into Boston, in fact Molly's father worked there, Molly and her friends rarely left their hometown of Chase. They could play on their small school's playground or on the town's ball field. There was a community pool to swim in during the summer. But everyone in Chase looked forward to the school carnival. There were lots of booths where people could sell their arts and crafts. There were booths where the children could play games like penny pitch and ring toss. There were booths where people sold delicious food like cookies, brownies, kettle popcorn and fried dough. Best of all, there was a big bounce around. The line for that was always the longest.

As she walked down the hallway toward the cafeteria thinking about the carnival, she heard someone calling her name. Turning slowly, she looked to see who it was.

"Unbelievable," Molly thought. It was Sue. She hadn't heard the girl say two words since kindergarten and now Sue was calling to her. First, she spoke to the teacher and now she was trying to talk to Molly. Molly thought about turning around and continuing on her way to meet her mother, but she was curious about what Sue would say. So she stopped.

Sue caught up to where she was in the hallway. Sue still looked angry.

"I just can't believe that Miss Bees could be so mean." Sue stammered.

"Me either," answered Molly. "Who cares about those stupid fast facts? I mean imagine having to miss recess for that."

"Oh, I didn't think Miss Bees was wrong about keeping us in for recess. After all, she did tell us she would do that," Sue replied. "But how can she keep Juan in. He can't even speak English so how would he even know that he is supposed to learn the multiplication facts."

Molly was stunned. Sue didn't mind missing recess.

"But what about your recess?" Molly inquired.

"I don't mind missing recess," Sue answered. "I don't have much fun outside anyway. The only time kids would play with me was when I used to have sashes and bows on the back of these dresses." Running her hand down to her waist, Sue continued, "But I had to cut them all off because the boys would untie them and pull me around the blacktop."

Molly noticed that there were small flaps of material on each side of Sue's dress. She vaguely remembered seeing Sue dragged around the blacktop back when they were younger.

Sue continued. "But the reason I tried to find you after school was that I wondered if, I mean I thought that, I mean that I hoped that maybe your mother could speak to Miss Bees about letting Juan out of the fast facts."

Molly didn't get past the part where Sue said she tried to find her after school. Didn't Sue take a bus home? Wouldn't someone be looking for her when the bus stopped?

"Why don't you ask your mother to do it?" Molly asked. "Or how about your father?"

"I don't have a father," Sue murmured.

"Why not?" Molly inquired.

"He's gone. It's just my mother and me now."

"Won't your mother wonder why you aren't on the bus?" Molly asked.

"I don't take the bus," Sue answered. "I'm a walker. I think Juan and I are the only ones. Haven't you ever noticed that we leave the classroom before the rest of the class at the end of the day?"

Molly shook her head no. She really hadn't ever noticed what the walkers did. She was usually packing up her backpack, which always matched her jacket. She looked back at Sue.

"Why do you think my mother would be able to get Miss Bees to change her mind about Juan?" Molly asked Sue.

"Your mother is an important lady in the town. She's running the school carnival. Miss Bees would have to listen to her."

"But, I don't think my mother would ask her," Molly answered regretfully. "She's always told me she won't interfere with what happens between my teachers and me."

"If someone else doesn't help, Juan will miss recess for the rest of year and he will never learn to speak English. We know Miss Bees will never help him. She never helps anyone. Even the rich kids."

"Miss Bees won't help Juan and she won't help us either," Molly said. "I think we are going to have to figure out how to get our recess back ourselves. Why don't you come over to my house and we can try to figure something out?" Molly could not believe what she had just said. She had invited wimpy Sue with the ugly hair and clothes to come to her house. If anyone ever found out, they would never play with her at recess again.

"You want me to come to your house?" Sue asked.

Molly pondered that question. She really didn't want to be seen with Sue but there was no one else to help her get her recess back. "Yeah, I do," she replied. "We just have to wait until my mother finishes this meeting. Do you need to call your mother and tell her where you are going?"

"She won't care," Sue whispered. I'm going to go sit over there and do my homework while we wait."

Molly was surprised that anyone would want to do their homework so soon after school finished. She liked to play for a while when she got home, but she thought she might as well get her homework done. She didn't think she would have much more conversation with Sue as she had already talked more than Molly could ever remember.

When Mrs. Plies ended the meeting, she walked over to where Molly and Sue were sitting. Molly introduced Sue to her and they went to their car for the ride home. Sue sat in the back and didn't say one word. After parking the car in the garage, Mrs. Plies opened the door into the kitchen.

"Oh, this is a beautiful room," Sue sputtered. "Look how clean it is and how everything matches."

Molly nodded her head. It was certainly true that everything matched and the house was spotless. Molly's mother prided herself in keeping a clean house where everything was in its place.

"Thank you, Sue," Molly's mother said. "It is so nice to have my work appreciated. Let me get you girls a snack and then you can get to work on your project."

Sue looked at Molly. Molly was relieved that Sue didn't ask what project. After serving the girls vanilla pudding cups that she got out of the refrigerator, Mrs. Plies explained that she had lots of reports to type from the meeting she had held that afternoon and excused herself to go to her home office.

"Thanks for not squealing to my mother about why we are really here," Molly said to Sue. "If my mother knew why I missed recess, I would be in big trouble."

"I wish my mother would even care," Sue said quietly. Perking up a bit, she then asked if Molly had thought of a way to get Juan back his recess. Molly shook her head no. Nor had she thought of a way to get back her own recess.

Sue bent down her head and looked like she was really thinking, thinking hard. After a minute or so, she lifted her head and explained that she might have a way to solve this problem. Molly was amazed. What could it possibly be?

"I think we are just going to have to memorize the multiplication facts or figure out a way to solve them."

"Yeah, right," Molly responded spitefully. "If I could do that, I would have done it already."

"But, maybe if we work together we could come up with most of the answers. Then we just have to hope that the facts we don't know aren't on Miss Bee's fast fact paper. How about we talk to Juan tomorrow and get him to help us?"

"What can he do? He doesn't even speak English!" Molly asked.

"Oh, I think he understands a lot more than he lets people know. Haven't you ever noticed that he looks at the person speaking and often shakes his head yes or no while they are talking? Like today when Miss Bees asked us if we understood that we had to learn those facts and he shook his head yes. If he didn't understand any English, he wouldn't have known whether to shake his yes or no or if he should shake his head at all."

Amazing, Molly thought. Sue was much different than she had ever thought. She could actually talk and she was pretty clever. For example, she noticed that about Juan. She would have to watch him tomorrow to see if what Sue said was true.

Mrs. Plies walked into the room as Molly was thinking about becoming a detective. She explained that it was getting late and she would have to drive Sue home so that she would have time to make dinner for Mr. Plies.

Sue tried to say that she could walk home, but Mrs. Plies would not allow that. Once again, Sue sat alone in the back seat of the car. Except for giving Mrs. Plies directions, she stopped talking.

Molly was surprised to see where Sue's directions lead her mother. She had never been on the street where Sue lived. In fact, she didn't even know that the street existed. Even more surprising was that there was a fairly large house at the end of the street and Sue said that she lived there. Molly would never have guessed that Sue lived in the house and a big house at that. She had never really given much thought to where Sue lived because she had never given much thought to Sue at all. However, the size of Sue's house shocked her. How could someone as poor as Sue who only had four or five dresses to wear to school all year, live in a big house?

Sue thanked Mrs. Plies for driving her home and ran into the house. Molly didn't get a chance to see what was inside the house or to see Sue's mother. While she was wondering what Sue's mother, Mrs. Tract, looked like, her mother interrupted her thoughts.

"What a lovely young lady that Sue is," Molly's mother exclaimed. "And did you see her dress?"

Molly was about to make a snide comment about how old and faded the dress was and how poor Sue had to cut the sashes off the side when her mother continued.

"I wonder who did the smocking on the dress. It was beautiful work."

"What's smocking?" asked Molly.

"Did you see how the top of her dress had little gatherings that were sown together in a pattern? That's smocking. Dresses like that cost a lot of money, as they have to be hand sewn."

Molly was shocked. She wondered where Sue could have gotten those dresses.

CHAPTER 3: TURN AROUND FACTS

On Tuesday morning, Molly had a surprise in her backpack. She couldn't wait to share it with Sue and Juan during recess. She was so excited about her surprise that she forgot she was mad at Addy when Addy got onto their bus and came and sat next to her. She wasn't even that upset when Addy asked her why she had to miss recess the day before. Molly explained that old Miss Bees wouldn't let her have recess until she could get all 30 facts right on the fast fact test. Molly was going to ask Addy how she had done it, but she already knew what Addy would say. Addy loved math lessons and never had any trouble. Molly knew that Addy would say that she just "saw" the answers. Molly also knew that wouldn't help her because she only saw the problems.

"But don't worry;" Molly continued telling Addy, "I'll be out at recess just as soon as we have another one of those fast fact papers. I figured out what to do."

Even though Addy begged her to tell what she was going to do,

Molly shook her head no. It was such a great solution; she didn't want to give it away.

All morning long, Molly worked on her worksheets. When she walked over to put them into the correct baskets, she smiled at Sue. Leaning down she whispered, "Don't worry, I solved our problem." She hoped no one in the class saw her talking to Sue.

Finally, the class left for recess. Miss Bees explained that after she took the class out to recess, she had to go to the office to get her mail. She told Molly, Sue, and Juan to practice their facts.

Juan started laughing just as soon as she left. Molly and Sue looked at him trying to figure out what he thought was so funny. He looked back at them. Bringing his hand up to his lips, he started to make puffing sounds. Sue started giggling too.

"What's he doing?" Molly asked Sue.

"He's showing us that Miss Bees is going to smoke a cigarette."

Juan nodded and started giggling again. Molly and Sue joined in on the laughter.

"I wonder how he knows that?" Molly inquired, but then she remembered the surprise she wanted to share with her two fellow recess detention classmates. She got up from her seat and walked back to the cubbies to get her book bag. Triumphantly she brought three small boxes back to the front of the room. She gave one to Sue and one to Juan.

"These are calculators. My mother buys me a new one each year at the beginning of school. I don't know why she thinks I needed so many," she announced very loudly. "We can use them to give us the answers on the next fast fact test. Then we won't have to miss any more recess."

"Molly," Sue said quietly, "you don't have to yell. Juan isn't deaf. He just speaks Spanish instead of English." Then Sue continued, "I don't think Miss Bees will let us use calculators."

"I don't care if she lets us or not. We can just sneak them."

Sue looked shocked. Juan shook his head back and forth.

"Molly, that won't work. First of all, it would be cheating. And Miss Bees will see us. We will be the only ones working on the fast fact

28

papers so she will be right on top of us with her stopwatch."

"Then what do YOU suggest?" Molly whined. "I told you that I can't learn those facts when I don't even know what multiplication is."

Like a jack-in-the box, Juan jumped out of his seat and ran to the front of the room. He grabbed a piece of chalk and wrote **3 x 4** in big numbers on the board. He turned back to see if the girls were watching. After he was sure they were paying attention, he drew three big circles and put four small squares in each circle. He walked to where he had written the multiplication fact and underlined the **3**. Jogging back across the front of the room, he underlined the three circles. He ran back to where the fact was and underlined the **4**. Quickly he returned to his picture and pointed to the four squares in the first circle, then the four squares in the second circle, and then the four squares in the third circle. Next, he counted aloud as he touched each square. "Uno, dos, tres, cuatro, cinco, seis, siete, ocho, nueve, diez, elevenio, and twelvio." Walking back to the multiplication fact, he finished the equation by writing "**=12**." Turning back to the girls, he bowed and returned to his seat.

Molly clapped her hands with delight. "So that's what it is. It's just like adding things together, but all the circles have the same number of squares in them. It's just three groups of four. " Turning toward Sue she asked, "Why didn't Miss Bees just tell us that?"

Sue looked perplexed. " Elevenio and twelvio," she whispered. But then she looked at Molly and replied to her, " I don't know why Miss Bees didn't just show us that. It makes sense now. All we have to do is draw Juan's pictures and we can get the answer to all the facts."

Sadly, Molly shook her head. "That's not going to work. We won't have time to draw all those pictures. I guess we are going to have to figure out a way to remember them all. How many facts are there? I think there are about a billion. I'll never be able to remember a billion facts."

"No, there are only 100," answered Sue.

"One hundred, " moaned Molly, "it might as well be a billion. I don't think I've ever learned 100 facts about anything."

Juan was up out of his seat again. Back he went to the front of the room. He took the chalk and wrote **4 x 3** underneath where he had written **3 x 4** a few minutes before. Again he drew circles. This time he drew four circles and drew three squares inside each one. Checking to make sure the two girls were watching, he counted out the squares again, ending his counting at "twelvio." He walked back to where he had written the new math equation and wrote "**=12**." Instead of bowing this time, he spun around and then took his bow.

"Why is he spinning around?" asked Molly.

"I get it," replied Sue. "He's showing us that multiplication has turn around facts. He's showing us that the answer to a problem like **5x7** would be the same as the answer to **7 x 5**. Remember we learned that in first grade about addition. If multiplication has turn around facts, we only need to remember 50 facts. See Juan has made are job easier already."

Juan smiled at what Sue was saying, but then looked nervous. He grabbed an eraser and quickly removed all of his work from the board and jogged back to his seat.

"O.K., this is better. Now we don't have to learn as much. But how are we going to do that?" inquired Molly.

Looking up at the clock, Sue noticed that recess time was almost over. "Could we meet after school and work on this some more?"

"I have to stay and meet my mother again in the cafeteria. Do you want to stay with me again?" asked Molly.

"I could do that. But what about Juan?"

"How do we ask him? He doesn't speak English."

Both girls looked at Juan, but he looked down at his desk.

Just as he looked down, Miss Bees opened the door and came into the classroom.

"Have you got all the facts memorized now?" she asked.

"Yeah, right," Molly mumbled. "I just have to remember 50 different things and then I can have recess. I may never have recess again."

"What are you saying?" Miss Bees snipped at Molly.

"Oh, um, we're working on them, Miss Bees," she responded.

The rest of the class came back from recess and the afternoon worksheets were handed out.

CHAPTER 4: ZEROES AND ONES

After school, Molly was really worried now that her mother and father were going to find out that she was missing recess and that she might have to miss recess until she graduated from high school. At the end of the day, she packed up her book bag and got in line to go to the bus. Then she remembered that she was supposed to meet her mother in the cafeteria again. She got out of the line and headed toward cafeteria where her mother was having another meeting. As she walked down the hall, she heard her name being called.

Turning around, she saw Sue. Molly wondered what Sue wanted. Then she remembered that they were supposed to meet in the cafeteria after school. She waited in the hallway for the slim girl to catch up to her.

"Wasn't it wonderful the way that Juan showed us what

multiplication is?" Sue gushed. "He's a <u>much</u> better teacher than Miss Bees."

As Sue finished her sentence, the girls heard a soft cough from down the hallway. Turning to look to see who was there, they were both surprised to see Juan.

Molly pointed to herself and then to Sue and then to the cafeteria. "Are you coming to meet us?" she asked the new boy.

Juan nodded yes and started down the hall to meet them. The three students walked into the cafeteria. Just as they entered, Mrs. Plies was putting on her coat.

"Molly," she called out. "I have to go into town to buy some poster paper to make signs for the carnival. Do you want to come with me?"

Molly didn't know what to do. Sue and Juan were waiting to meet with her to make more plans to escape from recess detention. She knew her mother wouldn't let them go to their house if her mother was in town. She knew that Sue could walk home, but she had no idea where Juan lived. It couldn't be too far away, because Sue said he was a walker. She felt badly that she wasn't going to be able to meet with

34

Juan and Sue but she guessed she would have to go with her mother.

"Hello, Mrs. Plies."

Who was talking to her mother, Molly wondered. It was Sue. That Sue was full of surprises. She never talked to kids but she could talk to grownups like Miss Bees and her mother.

"Mrs. Plies, I wonder if Molly could come home with me today so that we can work some more on our project?" Sue asked. "Oh, may I introduce our new classmate, Juan? He's going to help us."

Molly was stunned at how easily Sue talked to her mother. She was even more surprised when her mother agreed to let her go home with Sue. Usually, Molly had to make play dates a week ahead of time so that her mother could make sure it fit on her day planner. Her mother also called the other mother to confirm the arrangements.

"I'll just pick her up when I'm done doing my errands downtown. I really have to get the poster paper today or we will get off schedule preparing for the carnival," explained Mrs. Plies.

Now Molly understood. We could <u>never</u> get off schedule. Molly's mother didn't care where Molly was going because if she didn't get the poster paper that afternoon, her carnival schedule would be off. But, that was fine with Molly. If they went to Sue's house, they could talk about the fast fact test without Molly's parents knowing that she was missing recess.

Waving good-bye to Molly's mother, Molly, Sue, and Juan headed out of the school. "How do we get to your house from here?" Molly asked.

"We just take this shortcut," Sue said. She led them across the playground and up the hill behind the school. After walking through some trees, they arrived on Sue's street. Soon they were at Sue's house.

"Before we go in," Sue said shyly, "there is something you need to know about my mother."

Molly and Juan both looked at her. Sue looked like she might start to cry, but she raised her head and continued.

"My mother's been sick for a while. She pretty much just stays on the couch so our house isn't very tidy. We'll just walk through the living room and go to my room and work on those facts."

Sue opened the door to her house and led the trio in.

Molly was shocked. "Not very tidy" was not even close to the way Sue's house looked. There was stuff everywhere. Molly couldn't even see the chairs in the room or most of the rug because of the clutter. She looked at Juan, but he didn't seem to notice the mess.

"Mom," she heard Sue say. "I've brought some friends home from school to work on a project."

Molly looked to see to whom she was talking. Then she noticed Mrs. Tract. Mrs. Tract was lying on the couch covered with a tattered afghan. Molly could now understand why Sue had such ugly, stringy hair. Sue's mother's hair was worse than Sue's. Molly waited for Sue's mother to say something. She didn't.

Sue pointed to a stairway and led the group up the stair. When they entered Sue's room, Molly had another shock. Sue's room was very neat. Although everything in the room was a bit shabby, the room was clean and the bed was made. Molly wondered why Sue's mother picked up Sue's room but not the living room.

Sue moved a chair away from the old desk in the room and put it next to her bed. She pointed to Juan and he sat down in the chair. Then she indicated that Molly should get up on the bed. Walking back to the desk, Sue took out some paper and pencils and gave some to each of her guests.

"OK," Sue started, "Now we know what multiplication is..."

"Not that we will ever need to use it," interrupted Molly.

"Oh, we'll have to use it all right. We have to get the answers to those fast fact questions." Sue replied. "So, what facts do you know?"

"I know **3 x 4** and **4 x 3**," Molly said and turned to look at Juan. Juan looked embarrassed. "You did a good job of showing us that," Molly continued. Juan looked even more embarrassed. "What else do you know?" she asked the others.

"Let's start at the beginning. What about the zeroes?" Sue said. Then she drew a big **0** on her paper and showed it to Juan.

"Si, nulo," he said nodding. "Nulo es nulo."

The girls looked at him curiously. They shook their head to show Juan that they didn't understand. Juan then took his paper and wrote

0 x 4. Then he waved his hands to show he was finished drawing and pointed back at the zero in the problem.

"What's he doing?" inquired Molly.

"I think I get it," answered Sue. He's not drawing any circles because there aren't any groups. No groups of nothing is nothing. 'Nulo es nulo.'"

"I get it now and," Molly said triumphantly, "it would work the other way too. Four groups of nothing is still nothing. **4 x 0** is **0**. Zero's like the hero."

Molly started to giggle as she repeated the slogan " zero is the hero." Now that's a start, we've already learned ten facts—zero times the numbers one through nine."

"No," corrected Sue, "we've learned twenty facts—remember the turn arounds." Sue looked perplexed. "Or maybe just nineteen. I don't know if you get to count **0 x 0** twice."

"Who cares," Molly said. "It's a whole bunch more than I knew before. What's next?"

"I guess we look at numbers times one." answered Sue.

Once again, Juan was busy writing on the paper Sue had given him. When he finished he showed his work to the two girls. Sue was smiling as he turned it around. Molly guessed she already knew what would be on the paper. They were both right. Juan had written **1 x 6** and drawn one circle with six squares inside. Then he wrote **1 x 6 = 6**.

"Look how easy that is," said Sue. "Any number times one is the same number."

"It's like **1** is a mirror and the other number sees itself. One is the mirror. Even I can remember that. So now we know 20 facts—no that's not right. We know 40 facts. If mean old Miss Bees gives us a fast fact test with just the ones and zeroes on it, we'll get them all right."

Just as Molly was about to ask what they would do next, the children heard a grownup talking downstairs. Sue jumped up and ran toward the stairway. Molly and Juan followed her down the stairs. At the bottom of the stairs, Sue stopped and tried to straighten out her dress before she walked into the living room

"Hello, Mrs. Plies," she said, "Were you able to get everything you needed downtown?"

Mrs. Plies looked at Sue and then at Sue's mother who remained lying on the couch. Stuttering she said, "I knocked and knocked at the door, but no one answered. The door wasn't locked so I opened it to call for Molly. When I saw your mother I thought she must be ill. I was about to ask her if she was OK when you came into the room."

"My mother doesn't feel well. But she will be fine. Won't you mother?" Sue murmured. Mrs. Tract nodded her head, but still didn't speak. Turning to Molly and Juan, Sue thanked them for coming and started to walk toward the door.

Molly turned to Juan and said loudly, "Do you need a ride home?" Remembering that she didn't have to shout, she asked the question again more quietly. Juan shook his head. He held out his left hand flat and used two of the fingers from his right hand to make the motion of walking. Nodding at Sue, Mrs. Tract, Molly, and Mrs. Plies, he walked quickly out of the door and across the street toward the path through the little woods.

Molly started towards the door when her mother poked her in the arm. Remembering her manners, Molly thanked Sue and her mother and the Plies left Sue's house.

Molly went to their car. After attaching her seat belt, she turned toward her mother and waited. She was sure that her mother would have some kind of comment to make about the condition of Sue's house. Even Molly, who wasn't concerned about always having everything put away in its right place, thought that Sue's house was a mess. But Molly's mother surprised her.

"Don't you think that Sue such a nice polite girl?" asked her mother.

"Yeah," answered Molly. "What do you think is wrong with her mother?"

Mrs. Plies turned toward Molly to answer that question. As she turned, she almost hit the large black car that was passing them.

"I wonder who owns that limo," Molly's mother stammered. "Who could have moved into our town that could have that kind of car? I'll have to see if I can find out. Maybe they could give us something for the carnival." She paused, but then continued. "Speaking of the carnival, Molly, could you come after school and help make the posters we need to advertise our fair?"

Molly nodded that she would. She knew that once her mother started thinking about the carnival, she would never go back to Molly's question about Sue's mother.

CHAPTER 5: FIVES AND TWOS

Once they got back home, Molly went to her room to play computer games. Her mother would make dinner and then visit with her father when he got home from work. She also knew that she was not invited to visit with them. She could talk to her father during dinner—as long as she didn't say anything to upset him. Then after dinner, she was to go back to her room to complete her homework.

Her homework that night was easy. Miss Bees didn't give them much homework. All she had to do was write her spelling words three times. While she worked on writing her words, her mind drifted off to her meeting that afternoon with Sue and Juan. She thought it was great how Juan had figured out how to do the zero and one times tables. She wondered if she could figure out a trick for another set of facts. Her eyes drifted around her room. Her room was beautiful. Everything matched. Her bedspread looked like the blue sky with fluffy white clouds floating on it. Her rug was exactly the same shade of blue as the bedspread. The curtains at her window also looked like the fluffy clouds. She even had a fluffy cloud clock. Molly remembered how excited her mother was when she found it.

Molly also remembered that she was not as excited as her mother. The clock was the old fashioned kind of clock. It was a clock like they had in their classroom. In fact, it was a clock like the clock she saw in every room in her school. Molly liked the digital clock that her parents had in their room. It was much easier to tell time on a digital clock. In order to figure out how many minutes it was after the hour, Molly had to count by fives. Sometimes, when she was a little kid, she even had to put her pointer fingers on the numbers on the face of the clock. Molly took the clock off the wall and counted out the minutes: **5, 10, 15, 20, 25,** and **30**. When she reached the **6** at the bottom of the clock, it came to her. She was counting off equal groups of fives. Those numbers would be the answers to the five times tables. She was so excited that she had figured it out; she wanted to run and tell her parents. But she knew she couldn't. If she told them, they might learn that she didn't know her multiplication facts. However, she did know whom she could tell. She couldn't wait to get to school the next day to tell Juan and Sue.

The next day at school, Molly rushed through her morning work and was pretty quiet at lunch. Only Addy knew the real reason why she had been missing recess. Addy was a great pal and hadn't told their other friends. Once again Miss Bees brought the rest of the class out to recess leaving Molly, Sue, and Juan alone in the room. Once again Miss Bees did not come back to give them any help.

Molly was glad Miss Bees didn't return. She was anxious to explain to Sue and Juan the way she had figured out the answers to the five times tables. This time she went to the front of the room. She drew a big clock on the board and showed the other two how they could count by fives to figure out what **5 x 8** would be.

Juan and Sue seemed thrilled with her discovery. Sue even pointed out that the practice with the five times tables would also help them to learn to tell time more easily. Molly thought about telling them how she liked digital clocks better, but stopped when she heard Sue say that she had also figured out a trick.

"I figured one out last night too," Sue said triumphantly. Molly was surprised that the normally shy and quiet girl was getting so excited. "Remember how Juan drew the picture of the groups on the board," Sue said. "Last night when I was writing my spelling words, I thought about those groups. When I was writing the words the second time, I figured out that two times anything means two groups. Then I thought about the fact that two groups of the same thing are like the doubles facts we learned in first grade from Miss Trigg. You remember; the facts like **1 + 1**."

Molly interrupted her, "Miss Trigg was great. Her class was so much fun. I remember when we learned those double facts, she had Kaleigh and Kiley, the twins, stand in the front of the room and hold up their fingers to show us what number we were on."

"And Miss Trigg taught us that doubles poem." Sue continued. Sue started the poem and Molly joined right in.

"One plus one is two, say how do you do." The two girls shook hands.

"Two plus two is four, we will travel more." The girls acted out riding in a car with their hands being the four wheels on the side of the car.

"Three plus three is six, we will have a sip." They acted out taking a soda out of a six-pack and drinking a sip.

"Four plus four is eight, spiders are so great." They made their fingers into the eight spider legs and pretended to be frightened.

"Five plus five is ten, shall we start again." Giving each other high fives, they spun around to continue.

"Six plus six is twelve, a dozen is so swell." They counted out twelve eggs in imaginary egg cartons.

"Seven plus seven is fourteen, two weeks are really keen. They counted off two weeks' worth of days on a make-believe calendar.

"Eight plus eight is sixteen, red and blue and green." The girls made believe that they were taking sixteen crayons out of a crayon box that had two rows of eight.

"Nine plus nine is eighteen, that makes two baseball teams." The girls swung their arms as if they were holding baseball bats.

"And ten plus ten is twenty, I think we've done plenty." Laughing together, they bowed to Juan. He clapped and clapped his hands.

Hearing the noise of their class returning from recess, Molly quickly erased her clock from the board. She asked the others if they could join her again in the cafeteria after school. Both agreed to come.

CHAPTER 6: NINES

Molly, Sue, and Juan walked together to the cafeteria while the rest of the class went to get on the buses to go home. Molly continued to feel proud of herself because she had figured out how to do the five times tables. She noticed that Sue was smiling more than she had ever seen before. She didn't know what to think about Juan. He remained a mystery. When they arrived in the cafeteria, Mrs. Plies came right over to them and thanked them for coming to paint the posters.

Molly had forgotten all about the posters. She looked over to Sue and Juan, but they were busy taking off their jackets and putting down their book bags. Neither one was upset about having to paint posters.

"Hey," Molly said, "I hope you don't mind doing these posters. I forgot that my mother had asked me to do them. But we can still do the multiplication facts." The girls began to review the tricks they had for **0, 1, 5,** and **2**. They had just begun to repeat the doubles poem they had learned in first grade when Mrs. Plies called back over to them. She asked how the posters were coming along. Molly yelled back that they were fine and quickly passed out the paintbrushes and paint jars her mother had left on the table.

"How many posters are done?" they all heard Mrs. Plies yell.

" We're working on them," she yelled back to her mother. As she started to paint the letters on the poster in the bright red color her mother had selected, she began to think out loud. "So now we have a way to figure out the answers to the **0s, 1s, 2s,** and **5s**."

"Nueve" said Juan.

"What?" questioned both Molly and Sue.

"Mi mamagrande. Nueve." Juan pointed at himself and held up nine fingers. Then he put both of his hands flat on the poster paper.

"Numbero?" he asked the girls.

Molly didn't have any idea what the boy was doing, but Sue figured out that he wanted them to pick a number and she chose 6.

Juan started with his left pinkie and counted uno, dos, tres, cuatro, cinco, seis. Then he tucked the thumb of his right hand under his resting palm. Next he counted out the fingers that were to the left of the tucked under finger. Uno, dos, tres, cuarto, cinco. Taking his paintbrush, he painted the number 5 inside one of the letters Mrs. Plies had drawn for them to paint. Then he counted out the fingers to the right of his tucked in thumb, uno, dos, tres, cuatro. He painted a small four next to the five. Then he painted the whole multiplication fact.

9 x 6 = 54. He smiled.

"Does that work for every nine times table?" asked Molly. Juan nodded.

The girls were delighted.   They took turns picking numbers and trying Juan's nine trick. Two good things happened. Mrs. Plies' posters were painted and Molly, Sue, and Juan practiced the nine trick. It was Molly's turn to pick a number and Juan's turn to paint the answer. Molly picked **8** and Juan tucked under his eighth finger. He was about to paint **9 x 8 = 72** when the jar of red paint tipped over. Sue was able lift up the poster before the paint spilled on it, but Juan was not able to move quickly enough to prevent the paint from spilling down onto his pants. The girls tried to wipe it up, but the only succeeded in wiping the paint into the fabric of his pants.

Mrs. Plies sensed something was wrong and came over to help. She was able to get some of the paint off his pants, but Juan did not look upset. He just did that "walking fingers" thing and packed up his book bag and left.

Mrs. Plies said that it was time for her to take Molly and Sue home too as the meeting for the carnival was over. The girls also packed up to leave.

"Do you think that Juan will get in trouble for ruining his pants?" Molly asked Sue. "What will he wear to school tomorrow?"

"One of his other pair of black pants. He's got about ten different pairs."

"How do you know that? I thought he had one pair of pants and one shirt," Molly inquired.

"Didn't you notice that some of the shirts have a pocket on the front, some of the pants have trim on the back pocket? They're all different."

Once again Molly was amazed at how observant Sue was. She was still pondering Juan's wardrobe as they got into the car and her mother drove them to their homes.

CHAPTER 7: THREES AND FOURS

"Another day without recess," Molly thought as she boarded the bus to go to school. Addy again asked, "Will you be able to come out and play this afternoon?"

Molly answered "No. I don't know when Miss Bees is going to give us another fast fact test, but I am feeling better about multiplication and hope to go out to recess soon."

The morning passed by quickly. Lunch did too. Once again Miss Bees took the class out for recess and did not come back to help the three students.

"Isn't she supposed to watch us?" asked Molly.

"I think so," answered Sue. "I don't think we are supposed to be in here by ourselves. But it's better. We get more done without her. I had to help my mother with the laundry last night, so I didn't think of any more tricks. Did you?"

Before Molly could answer, Juan was on his feet again. Molly noticed that there was no red paint on Juan's pants. Sue was right about his clothes. This shirt was different from the one he had on yesterday. Juan went to board and wrote **3 X 6**. Instead of drawing the circles as he had done before, he wrote the addition problem **6 + 6 + 6**. He turned to see if the girls were following what he was doing. They were. Next he put a box around the first two sixes. **[6 + 6]** Above the box he wrote the number **12**. Turning back toward the girls, he acted out counting something.

"What's he doing?" Molly wanted to know.

"He's counting something," Sue replied.

Juan pointed back to the two sixes in the box and acted out counting again.

"I've got it," Sue exclaimed. "He's counting out the eggs from Miss Trigg's poem. Remember,' six plus six is twelve. A dozen is so swell'."

Molly smiled showing that she understood. "But what about the other six?"

Hearing her question, Juan held up six fingers. On the board he wrote **13, 14, 15, 16, 17**, and then **18**. He went back to his original number sentence and finished it by writing =**18**. **3 X 6 = 18.**

"I think I see it," Molly said. "When we have a number times three, we just have to think of the double fact and then count on one more set of that number. Let's try another. Let's try **3 x 7**."

"I'll do it," cried out Sue. "**2 x 7** is fourteen. That's the calendar one. Then I have to count on seven more." Holding up seven fingers she counted out **15, 16, 17, 18, 19, 20**, and **21**. "It's **21**. **3 x 7 = 21** That doesn't take too long either. We could do that on a fast fact test.

Molly surprised that others by running up to the board next to Juan. "That gives me an idea for the fours." She wrote a multiplication problem on the board just as Juan had done. Molly chose **4 x 7**. Then she wrote the addition number sentence that went with it: **7 +7+7+7**. Like Juan had done, she put a box around the first two 7s: **[7 + 7]** and wrote **14** above them. Then she put a box around the other two 7s: **[7 + 7]** and wrote **14** above that box. Next to her addition problem, she added **14 + 14** and got **28**. Returning to her original multiplication fact, she completed it by writing **4 x 7 = 28**. "It's the doubles doubled," she proclaimed.

```
14      14                          14
(7 + 7) + (7 + 7) =              +   14
                                    ‾‾
                         28
```

"It's the double doubles," Sue corrected her. "It's like that clapping game that you and Addy do on the playground. Sue began the chant, but then Molly quickly joined in.

"Double, double this this.

Double, double that that.

Double this. Double that.

Double, double this that"

They clapped their hands together matching the rhythm of the chant.

Juan still looked confused, but Sue showed him another example. She wrote **4 x 6**. Then she explained that would be four groups of six. Pointing to the first number sentence, she said, "The first two sixes would be **12**. Adding the other two sixes would also be **12**. Then we add together the two twelves and we get the answer of **24. 12 + 12 = 24**

Double, double."

Juan nodded his understanding. Molly watched him and realized that Sue was right about Juan. He did understand English. She wondered why he pretended that he didn't.

"What are you three doing?" Miss Bees asked them loudly. They hadn't heard her come into the room. After quickly erasing their work on the board, they returned to their seats.

Miss Bees walked to the front of the room and announced loudly that she needed to talk to them before she went to bring the rest of the class back to the room. She declared that she would be giving them their fast fact test the next day. She continued to explain that she hoped they were ready for it now, especially because she had given them all that extra help at recess.

Molly wanted to laugh. Miss Bees hadn't given them any help. However, Molly knew she would get into even more trouble if she laughed at her teacher.

CHAPTER 8: RETEST

All the next morning in school, Molly was nervous. She barely talked to Addy and her other friends during lunch. She knew that she and Sue and Juan would have to take their fast fact test when the rest of the class went out to recess. Feeling nervous about a test was new to Molly. She had never had any trouble with other tests. The fast fact tests had never bothered her before, because she hadn't realized that they were important. Now she knew they were important, very important. Molly knew that her parents would soon find out that she was missing recess if she didn't do well on today's test.

But Molly was pretty confident that she would do all right. After all, she now knew what multiplication was and she had a way to figure out all the answers, thanks to Juan and Sue. She quickly reviewed her strategies:

zero is the hero

one is the mirror

twos are the doubles

threes are the doubles then count on another set

fours are the double doubles

fives are the count by fives.

Molly smiled to herself when she thought about how she had

figured some of them out. And what was the other trick, she asked

herself. "Oh, yes. Juan's "Nueve" trick. She liked that one best of

all.

Miss Bees told the three of them to stay in the room and to get

ready for the fast fact test. She would be right back after she took the

rest of the class out to recess. Molly turned to Sue and Juan. "We're

going to do great on this," she told them. Juan smiled back at her. Then

she looked at Sue. Sue didn't look happy.

Sue said, "But what about the sixes and…"

The door banged open and Miss Bees entered. She walked swiftly

to her desk and picked up the papers and her stopwatch. "I hope you

are ready for this. If you don't get all thirty facts correct today, I don't

know what I am going to do. I guess I might have to keep you after school."

The thought of after school detention frightened Molly. She didn't know what happened there, but she knew it was bad and she also knew that her parents would have to find out. She tried to forget about that for the moment though. She knew she would have to pay attention to the fast fact paper.

Miss Bees walked around the room passing out the papers. As always the papers were face down. The teacher returned to the front of the room. With stop watch in hand, she announced loudly, "Ready, set, go."

Molly flipped over the paper and began. She scanned the first row. This was going to be easy.

3 x 5—She quickly counted 5, 10, 15. On to the next one.

0 x 7—zeroes the hero.

2 x 4—four plus four is eight.

9 x 9—she tucked under ring finger on her right hand and saw 8 fingers before the tucked finger and one after—**81**.

4 x 7—double, double. Let's think. **7 + 7 is 14** and then **14 + 14** is **28**. She remembered showing Sue and Juan that one.

1 x 9 is 9. She liked that mirror.

8 x 2—that's the same as **2 x 8. 16** she wrote remembering the crayon box.

Now it was on to the second row. She knew she had plenty of time.

6 x 7—What was their trick for the sixes? Oh no! They didn't have any trick for the sixes. That's what Sue was trying to tell her. She turned to look to see if Sue or Juan had gotten to that fact yet. She saw Sue wipe her eyes and knew that she must have.

"Young lady, turn around immediately. We do not allow cheating in the classroom!" Miss Bees screamed. Molly was crushed. Not only would she not pass this stupid fast fact test, now Miss Bees thought she was a cheater.

"Pencils up." Miss Bees yelled. Molly limply lifted her pencil. She only had gotten ten facts done. She knew she would be in big trouble with her parents now.

The sound of whimpering made her turn around. She saw that Sue was trying to hide the fact that she was crying. The door opened and the class came back into the room. Miss Bees swooped up their papers and went to talk to the recess aide. Molly jumped out of her seat and went back to Sue's desk.

"Come," she whispered to Sue. Sue followed her to the back of the room where their coats were hung. Juan joined them. He was carrying a tissue that he gave to Sue. Sue quickly dried her eyes.

"Hey, it's not so bad. So we miss a few more recesses," Molly said trying to cheer up Sue. Juan nodded and smiled at the girls.

"I knew we weren't ready," mumbled Sue. "And it was **6 x 7**. I hate six and seven."

Molly was surprised at what Sue had said. How could anyone hate two numbers? What was wrong with six and seven?

Miss Bees' loud voice interrupted their conversation. "Everyone get in the seats. I need to pass out this afternoon's work.

CHAPTER 9: FIRST STINKY FINKY

Molly had trouble concentrating on her work in the afternoon. She almost forgot that she was supposed to meet her mother in the cafeteria where her mother was having another meeting for the carnival. Walking down the hallway, she was surprised to hear footsteps behind her. She wasn't surprised that it was Sue and Juan.

"Are you all right now Sue?" Molly asked.

Sue nodded her head. She asked "Are you O.K. Molly?"

Molly shrugged her shoulders. "Miss Bees is going to call my parents and I'm going to be in big trouble."

"At least I don't have to worry about that," Sue replied. Juan nodded his agreement.

"Ah, Sue," Molly continued. "Can I ask you a question?"

Sue answered, "Yes."

"How come you were so upset about six and seven. I know we didn't have a trick for that one but you seemed really upset about those numbers."

Sue looked very downcast. "It was something my father used to say before he left us."

"He left? I thought you said he died," Molly interrupted.

"No, I said he was gone. My parents used to be so happy. But something happened to my mother, she wouldn't get off the couch. And our house got messier and messier. My dad tried to help clean up at first, but then he kept saying that our house was 'at sixes and sevens.' I didn't know what that meant but it must have been awful because he moved away. I've never heard from him since. I don't know why he was mad at me. I tried to clean things up. I always kept my room clean and neat."

Molly didn't know what to say. She wondered what the sixes and sevens had to do with Sue's dad and the reason he left. Although she didn't get to spend much time with her dad, at least she had one. She peaked over at Juan to see what he was doing. He looked very upset at what Sue was saying. Sue was right about him. He understood English.

Molly's mother came over to the small group. "I don't have anything for you to paint today," she told them. "I'll try and find another project for you to do on another day. It's so nice that you want to help."

Juan nodded and did that walking fingers thing once again. Sue also stood up and said she would leave too. Molly was left alone with her mother.

"Ah, Mom," Molly started. "There something that I have to..."

Just then Molly's mother turned away from her. She had heard some of the other members of her committee talking. She turned back toward Molly.

"What is it, dear?" she asked.

"Nothing, Mom," Molly answered. "You go to your committee meeting and I'll work on my homework."

Molly was quieter than usual at dinner that night. She even asked to be excused before the family had dessert. Retreating to her room, she tried to decide whether or not she should tell her parents that she had not passed the fast fact test. She wondered why she and her recess detention companions hadn't talked about facts like **6 x 7**. She tried to figure out how many facts they still had to learn. She made a chart of all the zeroes, then the ones, then the twos, and the threes, fours, fives, and nines. All that was left was the sixes, sevens, and eights. Molly wrote down all of the facts for those three numbers. Looking at those lists, Molly figured out that she did know the answers to some of the facts. Remembering Juan's spinning around at the front of their classroom, she was able to cross out all of the **6, 7,** and **8** facts with the numbers **0, 1, 2, 3, 4, 5,** and **9**. They would just be turn around facts. Molly looked at the paper now. There were only six facts left:

6 x 6

6 x 7

6 x 8

7 x 7

7 x 8

8 X 8.

Surely there must be a way to figure those last six facts.

She decided to see if she could figure out the answer to any of these problems. "Let's start with the first one," she thought. "I'll do **6 x 6**." First she tried to draw Juan's circles with the squares inside. Drawing six circles and then drawing six squares inside each one took a long time. Too long! Then she thought about how Juan had done the three times tables. She remembers that **6 x 6** meant **6** groups of **6**. She wrote out the math equation **6 + 6 + 6 + 6 + 6 + 6.** That would be the same as **6** groups of **6**. She circled the first two sixes and wrote **12** on top of the circle. Then she circled the next two sixes and wrote another **12**. Finally she circled the last two sixes and wrote a third **12**. On the side of her paper she added up **12 + 12 + 12** and got **36**. Well, she thought, that works. But she wondered how long it took her to work out that answer. Watching her cloud clock, she waited until the second hand got up to the top of the clock on the 12. She worked as quickly as she could she wrote out the addition fact that matched **6 x 8**. That fact meant **6** groups of **8**. She wrote **8 + 8 +8 +8 + 8 +8.** She circled every set of two **8s**. She remembered that **8+8** is **16** from the doubles poem. Next she circles the sets of two eights. **[8 + 8] + [8 + 8] + [8 + 8]** and wrote **16** on the top of each circle. Finally she added up **16 + 16 +16** and got **48.**

Triumphantly she looked up at the clock. It had taken 35 seconds to get that answer. This method was not going to work for the fast fact test. It took way too long!

Molly began to cry. She knew that she was going to have to tell her parents about the fast fact tests because she was never going to be able to do thirty multiplication facts in a minute. She would never get them all right in her whole life. Resting her head on her arms, her tears spilled onto the paper on which she had tried the new technique. Her bedroom door opened.

Molly turned, expecting to see her mother. But she was surprised. Instead of her mother, Molly's father was standing in her doorway.

"What's the matter, pumpkin?" he asked.

Molly didn't know what to say. She was so surprised to see her father and to hear him call her "pumpkin". He hadn't used that nickname for her in such a long time.

Wiping her wet eyes on her sleeve, she replied, "I'm in big trouble dad. But it will be OK. You can go back downstairs and finish unwounding."

"Un—whating?" her father inquired.

"Unwounding," Molly replied. "Mom said that I wasn't supposed to bother you when you come home from work because you need time to 'unwound.'"

"Oh, you mean 'unwinding'," her father answered with a bit of a chuckle. "Well, your mother's gone to another committee meeting and I guess I'm done 'unwounding'. Now tell me, what's the matter here. It's not like you to cry."

Molly told her father the whole story of how she been losing recess because she didn't know her multiplication facts. She said that she thought she was ready for the fast fact test that day, but she had failed it again. She explained how Miss Bees was making Juan take the test even though he was new and only spoke Spanish. She told him that Miss Bees hadn't done anything to help them. Then she showed him all of the strategies that Sue and Juan and she had figured out all on their own. Finally she told her father that Miss Bees was going to keep the three kids after school the next week.

"What did you do wrong today?" he asked when she finished her tale of woe.

"I didn't know **6 x 7**," Molly told him. "I have a way to do all the facts except some of the **6s** and **7s**, and **8s**.

"Ah, the Stinky Finkys. I remember that I had trouble with them back in elementary school too."

Molly was stunned. She could not imagine her father having trouble with anything. Her father was really smart. He was a lawyer. Then she recalled that her father had called the hard facts by a funny name.

"What did you call them?" she asked.

"The Stinky Finkys," he answered. "Back when I was in school and having trouble with those facts, my teacher told me that every year her students would do fine with multiplication until they got to the facts that had **6, 7,** and **8** multiplied to another **6, 7,** or **8**. Her students hated them because they got them wrong. She called them the 'Stinky Finkys.' My teacher gave this name to those multiplication facts we didn't like, so I guess Stinky Finky means facts that nobody likes. My teacher made up a little story for each of the six facts. The parts of the story matched the numbers in the problem and then the answer. Let's see if I can remember any of them."

Molly's dad paced around Molly's room. Turning toward her, he smiled and said, "I've got one. It is for **6 x 8.** It went this way.

Six times eight is forty-eight.

I know the answer.

I am great.

Isn't that amazing that I can remember that after all these years."

Molly nodded her head and repeated the short poem her father had remembered. "Six times eight is forty-eight, I know the answer, I am great. I get it. The problems and the answer kind of rhyme so she made it into a poem." Molly repeated the poem, "Six times eight is forty-eight, I know the answer, I am great. Can you remember any of the other ones?"

Molly's father shook his head no. But then he said, "I'll try to think of them. And Molly, don't worry about Miss Bees. I'll tell your mother about what happened. Your mother and I need to talk about how we can help you." After kissing Molly on the forehead, her father left her room

"Only five more Stinky Finkys to figure out," Molly thought as she turned on her television to watch her favorite Friday night show. She couldn't wait to tell Sue and Juan about the Stinky Finkys.

6 x 8

POEM

Six times eight is forty-eight.

I know the answer.

I am great!

CHAPTER 10: PARENT CONFERENCE

Molly was surprisingly happy when she entered her classroom on Monday. She immediately went to find Sue and Juan. She wanted to tell them that she might have come up with a way to master those last six facts. Miss Bees intercepted her path to the back of the room and sent her back to her seat. All morning long, she tried to find a way to talk to Sue, but Miss Bees kept them busy with worksheets. Finally at lunch, she looked all over the cafeteria and found Sue sitting by herself at a back table. After telling Addy and her other friends that she had to meet with the recess detention group, she found Juan, also by himself, and brought him to the table where Sue was sitting.

Sue was astonished when Molly and Juan joined her for lunch.

"O.K.," Molly began. "This isn't going to be so bad. I talked to my father over the weekend." Molly stopped talking and checked to see if the mention of her father had upset Sue. Sue waved her hand telling Molly to continue.

"O.K.," Molly went on. "So I talked to my father and told him all about how we've been missing recess and how Miss Bees didn't help us and I showed him all of our tricks and then he showed me a trick he had learned when he was in school. It's called the Stinky Finkys.

"The what?" asked Sue.

"Stinky Finkys," Molly answered back. She explained the origin of the name and then told them the poem her father had given her the night before. Then remembering the Juan only spoke Spanish; she asked him if it would help him. He nodded yes. Continuing, Molly asked the others if they would want to work on making up some more Stinky Finkys when they had to stay inside for recess that afternoon.

But they didn't have a chance to make up any Stinky Finkys at recess that afternoon. Miss Bees only kept them inside for a few minutes.

" First," she told them, "None of you passed the fast fact test. But I can't keep you after school this afternoon because the school has a policy that parents must be notified a day ahead if a student would be missing the bus." Molly thought about pointing out to Miss Bees that Sue and Juan were walkers, but wisely kept her mouth closed.

"So now," Miss Bees informed the threesome, " I will be calling all of your parents and asking them to come into school to meet with me."

She went on and on about how she had never had a group that hadn't mastered the fast fact test before and how ashamed of the children she was. Molly's thoughts drifted away from her ranting teacher. She thought about how glad she was that she had told her father what was happening the night before. Then Miss Bees sent them out.

All evening, Molly waited for Miss Bees to call her parents. The call came at about 8:00 p.m. Fortunately, Molly father had already explained the situation to her mother. Mrs. Plies answered the call and told Miss Bees that she would come to see her the next day. Then she added that Mr. Plies would also be coming.

Molly turned toward her father and asked, "Will you get into trouble if you miss work?"

"Don't worry, pumpkin, I'm one of the bosses at my law firm now. I really want to meet this Miss Bees. I'd like to hear her explain what she's been doing."

Molly wasn't sure if that was a good thing or a bad thing. She didn't sleep well and was grumpy the next morning.

On the bus to school in the morning, her friend Addy wanted to know if she was going to be able to go out to recess and if she was going to sit with her at lunch. Molly confessed that she might never get to go to recess again the entire time she was in Miss Bees' class, but that she would be back at her old table at lunchtime.

Once she arrived in the room, she just had a brief chance to talk to Sue. Sue confirmed that Miss Bees had also called her mother. She said that her mother was going to come to school for the meeting. Sue wasn't sure if she should be happy or sad. She was sorry that her mother had to come to school because she was messing up her math work, but she was also delighted that her mother was going to get off their couch. She told Molly that the only other time her mother left the house was once a week to go to the bank and to get groceries.

The girls looked for Juan. When he saw them together, he joined them back where the coats were hung. Molly began to ask him if Miss Bees had called his parents. However, she remembered that he was supposed to only be able to speak Spanish. She made her fist resemble a phone and held it to her face.

"Did Miss Bees call your house?" she asked.

Juan nodded yes.

"Are your parents coming to the meeting?" she continued. Juan shook his head no.

"Mi mamagrande es como," he answered.

Miss Bees' loud voice interrupted their conversation. The three students quickly went back to their seats. Morning worksheets were handed out.

Later that afternoon, Molly eyes checked out the clock for about the hundredth time. This is the longest day of my life, Molly thought. Although Miss Bees hadn't kept them inside for recess, Molly didn't have much fun outside. Her friend Addy had tried to cheer her up by showing her the new clothes her mother had bought for her dolls, but even that didn't work. When Molly looked around the playground, she saw that once again Sue was sitting on a bench. Juan was with her, but they weren't talking. The time after recess until the end of the school day seemed like it took a week.

Finally, Miss Bees lined up the other students to meet the bus. Molly asked if she could please go to the bathroom. She was so nervous she thought she might be sick. Sue joined her and agreed that she wasn't feeling so well either. Hearing footsteps in the hallway, the girls decided that their parents must have arrived and opened the door to go back to their classroom.

But it wasn't their parents. It was Juan and his mamagrande.

"Please, Mama Grande," they heard Juan saying to the attractive, elderly lady who was walking with him. "Please pretend that you can only speak Spanish."

"Dave," she responded, "you aren't going to be able to get away with this act much longer. I will have to tell your father soon what you have been doing."

"Just a few more weeks," the boy pleaded. "Then we will know if Dad's staying here. I promise I will tell everyone who I am in a few weeks."

"But won't your teacher know that I am not really Spanish?" asked the mamagrande.

"Miss Bees doesn't really care about any of her students or their parents. You'll see at this meeting. In my other schools, the teachers made me feel comfortable when I joined their classes. She didn't even try at all. So, please, just for a few more weeks, let her think that I can only speak Spanish."

As Juan (or was it Dave) and his grandmother turned the corner to go to their classroom, Molly and Sue scurried back into the bathroom.

"You were right all along, Sue!" Molly exclaimed. "He does understand English. He even speaks English. Who do you think he really is?"

But Sue didn't get a chance to answer. Miss Bees' booming voice called the girls back to the room. Before they had a chance to speak to Juan/Dave, the other parents arrived and Miss Bees began the meeting.

"I'm so glad all of you could join me. Your children have a terrible problem," Miss Bees announced to the assembled group.

"What problem would that be?" Molly's father asked. Molly wondered if Miss Bees knew that her father was a lawyer and was good at asking questions.

Miss Bees looked surprised. She obviously was not used to parents making comment when she called them into school for a meeting.

Stuttering some, Miss Bees replied, "They don't know their multiplication facts. They have failed all their fact tests."

"So, what have you done to help them?" Mr. Plies asked.

Now this really confused Miss Bees. Molly peeked at Sue and Juan, who were both as amazed as she was that Miss Bees didn't have an immediate answer and that she had stopped speaking so loudly.

"I have another question," a different voice quietly said.

Every eye in the room turned toward Mrs. Tract. Molly could not believe that Mrs. Tract was talking. She was also amazed at how pretty Mrs. Tract looked. She still had straggly hair, but the blouse she was wearing matched the pants she had on. The blouse had the funny pleating just like the dresses that Sue wore. She looked so much better than the time that Molly saw her on the couch.

Mrs. Tract continued. "How long has this problem been going on? Why weren't we notified when our children failed the first test?"

"Well," Miss Bees stammered. "I didn't want to bother you. I know you haven't been well, Mrs. Tract. Mrs. Plies had the carnival to worry about. And, Juan doesn't speak English."

"Did you try to tell any of us?" Mrs. Tract inquired. "And what are you doing to help Juan? Have you tried to find anyone who speaks Spanish who can translate for him?"

All eyes turned toward Juan and his grandmother. The elderly lady began to speak, but Juan rested his hand on her arm. She bowed her head and remained silent.

"He'll probably be gone soon," Miss Bees answered. Then whispering, she continued, "You know migrant workers don't stay very long in any one place."

Juan's grandmother sat up straight and opened her mouth, but once again Juan held her hand. She didn't have to reply, though, as Molly's father was speaking.

"Migrant workers! We don't have migrant workers in this part of Massachusetts. Did you check his records to see where he was from or what his parents did?"

"His records are in Spanish," Miss Bees replied haughtily. "But let's get back to the real topic of this meeting. Your children do not know their multiplication facts and you need to fix that. I will continue to keep them in from recess and give them extra help until they can pass the fast fact test."

"Like you've done so far," Molly mumbled. Realizing that she would probably get into even more trouble, she quickly shut her mouth.

Mrs. Plies spoke and her voice covered Molly's remark. "We will do our part to help our daughter, but Mrs. Tract was very right to ask you why we weren't notified before. Thank you for inviting us to this meeting." She stood up. Her husband, Mrs. Tract, and Juan's mamagrande also rose.

Obviously, from the look on her face, Miss Bees was not used to having other people control her parent conferences. She didn't say anything as all of the parents thanked her for the invitation and put on their coats to leave.

As they were walking down the hall, Mrs. Plies excused herself from her husband and daughter. She rushed down the hall to speak to Mrs. Tract who was walking with Sue.

"Hi," she said, "I'm not sure you remember me. I'm Molly's mother. We met when I came to your house to pick up Molly one afternoon." Mrs. Tract nodded, so Mrs. Plies went on. "I noticed that your blouse has the same kind of smocking that Sue's dresses have. Could you could tell me who did the smocking?"

"I did," answered Mrs. Tract quietly.

"You did beautiful work." Mrs. Plies responded.

Before Mrs. Tract could continue, Molly and her father caught up to the two mothers.

"Great question you asked Miss Bees," Mr. Plies said to Mrs. Tract.

Mrs. Tract smiled. Sue looked at her mother and then at Mr. Plies and then back at her mother.

Mr. Plies continued, "That Miss Bees should have informed us right away when our kids were having trouble." All the adults nodded in agreement.

"It was nice to meet you, Mrs. Tract," he went on. "Oh, and my wife is right about the beautiful job on the smocking."

Molly rode home quietly in the back seat. What a day this had been. First she had discovered that Juan not only understood English, but he spoke English just fine. Then her parents and Sue's mother hadn't been afraid of Miss Bees. What a day!

CHAPTER 11:   SECOND STINKY FINKY

Molly listened to her parents as she rode in the car. She waited for one of them to say how great is was that they were not afraid of Miss Bees. Her parents did not care about that.

They did care that Molly was not doing well in math. Her mother said that perhaps she was spending too much time working on the school carnival. Her father reassured her that there was enough time to work on the carnival and to help Molly. The carnival was only a couple of weeks away and Mrs. Plies could not quit the carnival committee now. He also reminded her about how much she enjoyed that work. Then her father said that perhaps he was spending too much time at his office. Mrs. Plies told him that perhaps they should both spend more time with Molly when he was home. They both agreed that this was a great idea.

Molly thought it was a great idea too. She just couldn't figure out what they could do in this new time together that would help her learn those multiplication facts. She would find out that night after dinner.

Once dinner was done and the dishes were in the dishwasher, Mrs. Plies got things organized. She went into her office and came back to the dining room table with paper, file folders, markers, and pencils. Molly and her father smiled at one another. They were used to seeing Mrs. Plies getting things organized.

"So, let's make a chart of all of the multiplication facts and then we can color in all the ones that you know," Mrs. Plies said.

Molly was going to tell her mom that she had already done that but determined that it would be easier if she just let her mother lead the conversation. Mrs. Plies listed all of the facts. She started with the zero times tables and went right on through the nine times tables. Turning to Molly, she asked which facts she knew. Molly explained all of the strategies that Sue, Juan, and she had discovered. After each trick was explained, her mother highlighted those facts with a yellow highlighter. When she was done, those same six facts were left.

"Those are the 'Stinky Finkys,'" Molly pointed out to her mother. She told her mother the information that her father had told her. Then she repeated the poem for the **6 x 8** fact. Molly's mom loved the poem. She was also excited about the idea of the Stinky Finkys. She told them both that she wished one of her teachers had told her about the Stinky Finkys when she was in school.

But then Molly told her that her father couldn't remember any of the other stories.

"Not even one more?" her mother asked her father.

"Not even one," he answered disappointedly.

"Then we will just have to make up our own," she replied.

"How will we do that?" inquired Molly.

"I think we need to look at the factors and the products to see if we can think of something that goes with them." Mrs. Plies continued.

"What are the' factors' and the 'produce'?" Molly wanted to know.

"'Products'," Mrs. Plies corrected. "Didn't Miss Bees even tell you that the names of the numbers you are multiplying are the'factors'and the name of the answer is the ' product'?"

"Nope," Molly replied. "She just handed out worksheets."

"I guess that's my first lesson then," Mrs. Plies said. Then taking out a new sheet of paper, she listed the six Stinky Finky facts and their products.

6 x 6 = 36

6 x 7 = 42

6 x 8 = 48

7 x 7 = 49

7 x 8 = 56

8 x 8 = 64

Then next to the fact **6 x 8 = 48** she wrote the word " POEM." "One down, five to go," Mr. Plies said. They all looked at the list.

"Are any of the others coming back to you?" Mrs. Plies asked Mr. Plies. He shook his head.

Molly, her mother and her father studied the list. Then Mrs. Plies smiled.

"You probably don't know this Molly," she explained, "but while your father was learning to be a lawyer, I was learning about history. I especially liked American history. Looking at all the numbers on our sheet, the number that stands out for me is **49**."

"What's so special about **49**?" Molly wanted to know.

"There was a group of people in our country who were called the Forty-niners."

Molly was intrigued. Who were they, she wondered. Her mother was busy drawing something on another sheet of paper. When she turned it toward them, Molly's father asked if it were a map of the United States.

Molly's mother smiled. "I'm glad you figured that out," she said to her husband.

"Now, Molly," Mrs. Plies continued. "Pretend that it is the year, 1848. Now we live in this part of the country." She put a dot on the spot where their small town in Massachusetts would have been. "Things weren't good here at that time. There were many people out of work." Then she put a mark on the other side of the map. "But way over here, something exciting was happening. Not many people lived in this part of the country then. Some men were building a lumber mill and one of them saw something shiny in a stream. Can you guess what it was?"

Mr. Plies began to answer, but the quick look from his wife told him that it was Molly who was supposed to give the answer.

Mrs. Plies gave her another hint. "It was shiny and yellow."

"Gold! it was gold!" Molly shouted excitedly.

"Right," said both her parents together.

Mrs. Plies continued. "Once people found out that gold had been found in those hills, the word spread across the country. People started to leave where we live and journey across the country to find gold."

"Did they fly on a plane?" Molly asked.

"There were no planes then, pumpkin," her father explained. "Some went by ship around South America. Others had to go by wagon or by horseback."

"All the way across the country!" Molly was shocked.

"All the way," her mother went on. "And it was a hard trip. They had to get across the Mississippi River." She drew the river on the map.

"And across the Rocky Mountains." She drew the mountains on the map. "By the time they got to where the gold was it was 1849. Therefore, all the people that went to find gold were called the Forty-niners. There were thousands of them."

"Did they all find gold?" Molly wanted to know.

"No," her mother explained, "but most of them didn't want to make the long trip back so they stayed there. Before the Gold Rush, there had been a town near where the gold was found. Because of all the Forty-niners, it turned into a big city. It's called San Francisco now."

"And they have a football team that is called the Forty-niners. They wear gold helmets like the gold that was found there," Mr. Plies added to the story.

"That was a great story, Mom," Molly told her mother. "You're a better teacher than Miss Bees. She never would have made that part of social studies so interesting."

"Thank you Molly," her mother replied. "But right now we're worried about math. How do you think we can use my story to help you remember the **7 X 7 is 49**?"

The three Plies all looked at the fact on Mrs. Plies sheet. It was Mrs. Plies who came up with the solution.

"I know, I know," she exclaimed with glee. "Isn't seven said to be a lucky number? Just think how much luck you would have if you had **7** groups of **7**. **7 + 7 + 7 + 7 + 7 + 7 + 7**. You would surely find gold with all those sevens."

Mr. Plies then said, "Seven also works for the San Francisco Forty-niners. When you score a touchdown you get six points and then you get to kick an extra point and that's worth one. Six plus one is seven. Lucky sevens again."

Molly's mother went back to the list of Stinky Finkys. Next to **7 X 7** she wrote "Lucky Sevens."

"Two down and four more to go," said Molly.

"But those will have to wait until tomorrow," her mother explained after looking at the clock. "You still have to do your homework. You better do a good job. I don't think Miss Bees is too happy with you now."

Molly agreed. After thanking her parents and giving them each a kiss, she went to her room to do her homework. Spending time with both her parents reminded her of the summer evenings when they would all watch baseball games together on TV. Summer was a long way off, but she had another Stinky Finky to share with Sue and Juan— or was it Dave.

7 x 7

LUCKY SEVENS

49ERS: GOLD MINERS OR FOOTBALL TEAM

CHAPTER 12: THIRD STINKY FINKY

The next morning, Molly was nervous again as she rode the bus to school. She had enjoyed the parent conference the day before because Miss Bees seemed so uncomfortable. But now she had to go back to Miss Bees' class without her parents. When Addy asked her if she was in big trouble, Molly just shook her head. However, she told Addy that she didn't think that she would be going out to recess.

Molly tried to get to talk to Sue all morning. She wanted to tell her about the new Stinky Finky that her mother had created. She also wanted to ask Sue what they should do about Juan/Dave. She never got the chance.

Miss Bees didn't do anything unusually mean to them, but Molly, Sue, and Juan all knew that she wasn't happy with them. Then their teacher announced to the whole class that the three of them had to stay in at recess because they didn't know the multiplication facts. Molly was glad she had already told Addy, but was embarrassed when everyone else looked at her. At lunch, Molly didn't even start to sit at her regular table. She went straight back to the table at which Sue was sitting. Juan joined them.

"Don't you just hate Miss Bees?" she asked the other two. "I was so embarrassed when she told the whole class we had failed."

"I think they had already figured that out, Molly," Sue said calmly. "Besides, let's not worry about the rest of the class. We need to worry about ourselves now." Sue turned toward Juan.

"Is there something you want to tell us, Dave?" she whispered.

Juan/Dave looked shaken. "How did you find out," he whispered back.

"We heard you in the hallway when you were talking to your mamagrande," Sue explained.

Juan stood up and started to walk away.

"Hey, wait," Molly whispered at him. "You can't leave now. I have another Stinky Finky to show you and we need you to help us figure out the rest."

While Juan was sitting back down, Sue told him that they wouldn't give away his secret. Molly told him that Sue had figured out that he could understand English the week before. He told the girls that he could tell them the whole story in just a few more days and thanked them for keeping his secret. Then, he had another surprise for them.

Still whispering, he explained that he had been thinking about Molly's Stinky Finkys.

"I thought one up. It's the one for **6 x 6**. I wish we were back in the room. It works better when you can see it. Here's the idea. **6 x 6** is **36**. When I looked at it, I saw a lot of **6**s. There is only one other number in the fact. I figured out a way to remember it. Watch this.

Juan repeated the fact **6 x 6 = 36**. Each time he said a **6**, he held up a finger. Then he asked the girls how many **6**s were in the fact. The girls answered **3**.

"That's right, **3** sixes. Thirty-six. What I did was write **6 x 6** equals a blank and then a six. **6 x 6 = [ ] 6.** Then I filled in the blank with a three and created the number thirty-six." **6 x 6 = [3]6.**

"Great job, Dave," Molly said.

"Shush," Dave and Sue answered.

"I think you better just keep calling me Juan until I can tell everyone who I am."

During their indoor recess, Juan showed the girls his trick for **6 x 6** on the board. He was right. It was so simple when he wrote it for them to see. Then it was Molly's turn. She drew the map of the United States just as her mother had. Next she told them the whole story of the Forty-niners. Juan especially liked the part about the football team. Sue told Molly what a great job she had done. They just had enough time to erase the board before Miss Bees brought the class back into the room.

While handing out the afternoon worksheets, Miss Bees commented, "What a lovely spring day it is! It is too bad that everyone wasn't able to go outside and play. Molly began to get upset, but then she remembered that Juan had shown her another Stinky Finky. Now they only had to figure out three more.

6 X 6

MISSING NUMBER

6 x 6 = _____ 6

How many 6s

CHAPTER 13: FLASH CARD PRACTICE

Because there was no carnival committee meeting that afternoon, Molly took the bus home. Her friend Addy was very supportive. They both agreed that Miss Bees was going out of her way to make sure that everyone knew that Molly had to miss her recess because she hadn't passed the fast fact test. They also agreed that wasn't very nice of Miss Bees.

"What are you going to do about it?" Addy wanted to know. "Are you going to tell your mother?"

Molly explained that her mother already knew what was going on. Besides what could her mother do? Miss Bees was the only fourth grade teacher in their school.

Molly thought about complaining to her mother as soon as she got home, but decided to tell her about Juan's new Stinky Finky instead. Molly's mother was delighted with the discovery that Juan had made. She was on her way to her office to bring out all of the materials she had used the night before, but she changed her mind. She told Molly to go and work on her homework, because her father had called and said that he had something to show them after dinner

"But don't you have to go to a carnival committee meeting tonight?" Molly asked.

"I rescheduled it for tomorrow after school. You need to remember to meet me in the cafeteria," her mother replied. After giving Molly milk and cookies, she sent her off to work on her homework.

Molly finished her spelling homework in time to watch some television. She listened for the sound of her father's car pulling up the driveway and into the garage. As soon as she heard it, she ran downstairs to tell her father about Juan's new Stinky Finky and to find out what his surprise was.

Arriving at the bottom of the stairs, she remembered her mother's command to give her father time to unwind. She didn't have to. Her father came looking for her. He told her he remembered something else from when he was learning the Stinky Finkys that might help her and that he would show it to her after dinner.

Molly wanted to rush through dinner, but her parents made her slow down and eat her food. She did rush through the cleaning up process, but her parents seemed eager to get to her father's surprise, too.

As soon as the table was cleared, her mother assembled all of the Stinky Finky materials on the dining room table. Her father asked if she had any 3 by 5 cards. Mrs. Plies smirked and went back to the office and returned with 3" by 5" cards, 4" by 6" cards, and 5" by 8" cards. Molly and her father looked at each other. They both knew that he should have known better. Of course, Mrs. Plies had 3" by 5" cards.

First of all, Mrs. Plies took out their list of the Stinky Finky facts. She asked Molly to reiterate the two Stinky Finky stories that they already knew. Then Molly explained the new fact story that Juan had discovered. She wanted to tell her parents what she and Sue had discovered about Juan, but decided that his secret should be a secret from everyone as long as no one was going to get hurt by it.

Just as she was thinking about Juan, her father made a remark about him. He asked her mother if she knew Juan's parents. Her mother explained that Juan was new to town. Her father remarked that there was something about the way Juan looked that was familiar.

Mrs. Plies didn't agree. She didn't know anyone who looked like Juan, but she did like Juan's Stinky Finky. They decided to call it "the Missing Number."

Mrs. Plies filled that into their chart.

6 x 6 = 36 The Missing Number

6 x 7 = 42

6 x 8 = 48 POEM

7 x 7 = 49 Lucky Sevens

7 x 8 = 56

8 x 8 = 64

The three Plies studied the chart, but after a few minutes decided that they weren't going to be able to make up a new Stinky Finky that night.

Mr. Plies wanted to share his remembrance from when he was in school. He explained that his teacher had shown them how to make special flash cards.

Molly wanted to know what flash cards were. Smiling, her mother brought out a box of the cards. She told them that she had bought the cards that afternoon when Molly's father told her he was going to show Molly the special flash cards. Then she encouraged her husband to continue his explanation of his Stinky Finky flash cards.

Mr. Plies opened the package of flash cards that her mother had purchased and showed Molly what they were. He held up one that had **5 x 8** on the front and then turned it over so she could see that it had

 5 x 8 = 40 on the back.

"Now that's a regular flash card, but the Stinky Finky cards are different. We have to make them ourselves. They look like a regular flash card on the front, but on the back we draw a picture or write something like the poem. The picture or poem will remind us about the Stinky Finky. Then we should be able to remember the product.

Molly couldn't wait to make her Stinky Finky cards. Her parents checked her spelling of the words of the poem for their first Stinky

Finky, **6 x 8**. They decided that she should draw a pot of gold for the second Stinky Finky, **7 x 7**. For Juan's fact, **6 x 6**, Molly wrote

6 x 6 = ___ 6 on the back.

Molly enjoyed making the Stinky Finky flash cards but she wondered what she was supposed to do with them now that they were made. Her father showed her. He explained that she should turn the three cards so that just the problem side was showing and then stack them up. Then she should look at the first card. If she knew the answer, she got to put it in her winner's pile. If she didn't know the answer, she should turn the card over and look at the Stinky Finky clue.

Molly was anxious to try that out. Her parents stayed with her while she tried using her cards. The first time, she only got two of the facts correct: **6 x 8** and **7 x 7**. She forgot Juan's trick. As soon as she peaked at the back and saw the **6 x 6 = ____6** she remembered and announced it was **36**. The next time through she got all three facts right. She did that again for a third time.

Both Mr. and Mrs. Plies were delighted for her. Then, Mrs. Plies explained that Molly could use the regular box of flash cards in the same way. She could start with the pile showing only the problems. If she could say the answer to the fact and she was right after checking on the back of the card, that card went into her winner's pile. If she couldn't figure out the answer, that flash card went into her "Need to Practice" pile.

Her parents continued to watch her. Molly explained what strategy she was going to use for each fact. Again, her parents were impressed that she and Juan and Sue had figured out those tricks. Molly went through the whole box of flash cards. Her winning pile was huge. Her "Need to Practice" pile only had three cards in. None of the Plies were surprised when they reviewed those cards: **6 x 7, 7 x 8**, and **8 x 8**. Once again, it was those Stinky Finkys that were the problem.

It was Molly's mother who realized how late it was. Sending Molly off to get ready for bed, her mother asked her to call down when she was prepared to go to sleep. Molly wondered why. When she was about to get into her beautiful bed, she called. Both her parents came upstairs. Her father had brought up one of Molly's favorite books. He asked her if she thought she was too grown up to have her parents read her a bedtime story. Molly said she wasn't. In fact, Molly thought as her parents took turns reading, she didn't think she would ever be too grown up for a good bedtime story.

CHAPTER 14: FOURTH STINKY FINKY

Molly had a real surprise in her backpack when she headed off for school on Thursday. This time she was willing to share the whole story with Addy. She told her all about the Stinky Finkys and showed her the cards that her parents had helped her make. Addy was happy that Molly was in a better mood.

Molly told Sue and Juan that she had lots to tell them at lunch and that she had something great for them to do during their missed recess. Once again it was a beautiful spring day, but Molly didn't mind that she wouldn't be able to play outside. Even though Miss Bees continued to make nasty remarks about the three "failures," Molly stayed in her good mood.

At lunch, Molly told Juan and Sue all about the Stinky Finky flash cards and the way her mother showed her how to practice with the store bought cards. She also explained that her mother had given her enough cards so that Juan and Sue could make a set of Stinky Finky cards, too. They both were pleased that Mrs. Plies had thought of them. She told the others that they could make the cards during their missed recess time.

"Do you have enough for us each to make four cards?" Juan wanted to know.

"Sure," Molly replied, "Mom gave me enough cards for us to make all six Stinky Finky facts and some extras in case we make a mistake. Why did you want to know if we could make four cards?"

"Cause, I figured out another Stinky Finky," he answered.

Both Sue and Molly wanted to know which one. He told them it was the fact **7 x 8.** Then he went on to explain that he was looking at the numbers in the whole multiplication number sentence: **7 x 8 =56.** He asked the girls if they saw anything interesting about those numbers. They didn't.

"Let me give you a hint," Juan told them. "Think of counting, just regular old counting like everyone learns in kindergarten."

Molly and Sue both started counting. When they got to **5, 6, 7,** and **8**, Sue had figured it out.

"Look Molly," she said excitedly. "The problem has the numbers in order just like when you count, except that when you write **7 x 8** is **56**, its backwards. But we can remember **7** and **8** and then the **5** and **6**.

"That's another good one, Juan."

Juan blushed and thanked her.

None of the trio was upset when the rest of the class left for recess. They weren't even upset when once again Miss Bees made a big point about the fact that everyone else could go outside and play on the lovely spring day. They weren't surprised when Miss Bees did not come back to the room to help them.

First, Molly showed Juan and Sue the cards she had made. Next, she showed them how her father taught her how to use them. She showed them how to make the "Winner's pile" and the "Need to Practice" pile. Finally, she gave them each a set of 3 by 5 cards so that they could make their own set of Stinky Finky flash cards.

Each of the three students made a card for Juan's newest fact first. They wrote **7 x 8** on the front. Juan figured out how they could show his trick on the back. He suggested that they write the numbers from **0** to **9** just like a number line. Then they should underline the **7** and **8** and write a times sign between them. To finish the card they should put a box around the **5** and **6** and put an equal sign after the box. Molly wondered if you could write a fact with the answer first. She told the others she would ask her parents.

    1 2 3 4 (5 6) = 7 x 8 9

They didn't have time to finish all of the other cards before the class came back from recess. Molly suggested that they meet her in the cafeteria after school and they could finish them then. Sue and Juan agreed.

7 x 8

NUMBER LINE

1 2 3 4 [5 6] = 7 X 8 9

CHAPTER 15: FLASH CARD PRACTICE II

As soon as Miss Bees announced that it was time for the walkers to leave, Molly, Sue, and Juan left their room and went to the cafeteria. Mrs. Plies and her committee members were hard at work creating the decorations and signs that would go on the booths at the carnival. Seeing the children entering the room, she excused herself from the others and went over to where the children were taking off their jackets and their backpacks. She told Juan how much she liked his Stinky Finky for **6 x 6**. Juan nodded his thanks. Then Sue told Molly's mother about the new Stinky Finky that Juan had shown them when they had to stay inside for recess that afternoon.

"I like that one too, Juan," Mrs. Plies stated. "I brought both you and Sue something." She went back to where she had put her coat and reached into the large bag that she always carried for her committee work.

Returning to where the children were waiting, she gave Juan and

Sue a box of store-bought flash cards. They were just like the ones that she had given Molly the night before.

Thank you, Mrs. Plies," Sue said. Juan nodded his head.

Molly then reminded the others that they had to finish their special Stinky Finky flash cards. The children got to work.

About an hour later when the three students were each practicing their facts with their Stinky Finky flash cards, Mrs. Plies called over to say that the meeting time was over and asked Juan and Sue if they would like a ride home. Sue thanked her for the offer but said she could walk home. Juan nodded showing that he could walk too.

After the other two children left, Molly helped her mother clean up the tables in the cafeteria. As they walked together to their car, Mrs. Plies spotted that big black car again. "Molly, did you see that car?" she inquired.

"I did, Mom," Molly replied. "Let's wait here for a minute and see where it goes."

They were both very surprised to see the car turn down the driveway of the school. They were even more surprised when they saw

Juan come out from the main doorway of the school and walk over to the car. Juan got into the car and it drove away.

"Was that Juan?" Molly's mother asked her.

"I don't know, Mom," Molly answered. She would have to tell Sue all about the long black car in school the next day. Their friend Juan was certainly mysterious.

Molly forgot all about Juan and his mysterious car as soon as her father came home from work. He told the two women in his family that he had another great idea of how Molly could learn her multiplication facts.

As soon as the Plies finished dinner and the dishes were done, Molly and her mother returned to the dining room so that Mr. Plies could show them his new idea. Molly told him about the new Stinky Finky that Juan had figured out for **7 x 8**. Mrs. Plies took out the chart for the Stinky Finkys and added the trick for **7 x 8**. They decided to call it Number line. Mrs. Plies showed Molly the chart. They only had two more to figure out.

6 x 6 = 36 The Missing Number

6 x 7 = 42

6 x 8 = 48   POEM

7 x 7 = 49   Lucky Sevens

7 x 8 = 56   Number Line

8 x 8 = 64

Mrs. Plies remembered, "I have to make a phone call. I will be right back. I have to call the company from which the bounce around was rented to make sure that they will set up the large trampoline-like contraption about one hour before the carnival was supposed to begin."

While waiting for Mrs. Plies to return, Molly and her father reviewed all of the Stinky Finky stories. When Mrs. Plies came to the dining room a few minutes later, she looked a bit upset.

"No one answered the twenty-four hour phone number at the bounce around company," she explained. She asked Molly to remind her to call the company the next day.

Then Mr. Plies took over. He said, "I was thinking about the store-bought flash cards that your mother had bought yesterday. We have

one way to use them, but I thought of way that would be more fun. We

could play 'War.' "

Mrs. Plies looked shocked. Then she looked angry. "You know I

don't approve of violence," she snapped at her husband.

Laughing a bit, he responded, "It's a card game, dear."

Mrs. Plies apologized for snapping at her husband and listened to

his explanation of how the game worked.

"We each get an equal pile of cards. We put them so that the fact

side shows. We each show the top card on the pile. Then we take turns

saying the answer to our problem. Whoever has the highest answer

wins the cards of the other two. That person puts the three cards on

the bottom of the pile. We can play until someone wins all the cards or

we can play for a certain amount of time and see who has the most

cards."

"Let's play until someone has all the cards," Molly chimed in.

"I think we better just play for an hour tonight," her mother

replied. I think Molly should give all of the answers. Your dad and I can help you if you get stuck or if you make a mistake. That way you will get lots of practice."

The three Plies played "War" for an hour. Molly was delighted with the new game and wasn't even upset that she hadn't won. Well, not too upset. She couldn't wait to show Juan and Sue the game the next day. And she couldn't wait to tell Sue about Juan's car.

CHAPTER 16: TENS

Friday was another beautiful spring day in Chase, Massachusetts. Molly knew that she would still be missing recess, but she also knew that she had something fun to do indoors. At lunch, she sat with Sue and Juan. She told them all about the game that her father had shown her.

Juan told them, "I played that card game with my father. Each of us would flip over a card and whoever had the highest card would win the other card."

"How will that help us learn multiplication?" asked Sue.

"We weren't trying to learn any fact when I played with my dad," Juan told them. "We just played for fun." Pausing to think, he then said, "But you could learn multiplication facts. All you would have to do is give each person two cards. Then each player would multiply the numbers on the two cards and whoever had the highest answer would win all the cards."

"There would be lots of cards," Molly added.

Sue wanted to know what the cards with the pictures on them were worth. Molly told her that they would be worth 10.

"Do we know how to multiply by ten?" Sue inquired.

"That's an easy one," Dave told her. "All you have to do is count by **10s**. It's just like Molly's trick for the 5 times tables and counting by **5**.

While they ate their lunch, the three children took turns picking numbers and multiplying them by **10**.

When it was time for recess and the rest of the class had gone outside, Juan had two surprises. The first one was something he had forgotten to give the girls at lunch.

"My mamagrande made some cookies for us. They're called Mexican Wedding cookies. They're my favorite treat. He opened the bag of cookies and carefully passed them out so that they each received the same number of cookies. The girls agreed that they were delicious.

"What's your other surprise?" Molly asked as she wiped some powder sugar off of her face.

"It's something I figured out when we were practicing multiplying by **10**s at lunch, but I didn't have a chance to tell you. There's an easy pattern to the **10**s facts. Pick a number."

Sue picked 4. Juan went to the board and wrote **4 x 10**. Then he asked the girls to count by **10**s with him. They counted **10, 20, 30**, and **40**. Juan wrote the **40** after the fact. Then he showed the girls that the **4** in the problem matched the **4** in the answer.

$$\underline{4} \times 10 = \underline{4}0$$

"Does it always work?" Molly wanted to know. "Let try **7**."

Juan wrote **7 x 10** on the board and the three children counted out **10, 20, 30, 40, 50, 60**, and **70**. Sure enough, the **7** in the problem matched the **7** in the answer. All you had to do is rewrite the number from the problem and write a zero after it.

$$\underline{7} \times 10 = \underline{7}0$$

"That's really fun, Juan. I wish Miss Bees would give us some number times **10** on our fast fact test, but the fast facts are only from zero to nine."

"She probably doesn't give us any 'times **10**s' because they would be easy," Sue said. "Hey, let's play Molly's war game. We can use my flash cards. I have them right here in my desk."

Sue passed out the cards and the three children were happily playing war, when the door opened. It was Miss Bees. It was an angry Miss Bees.

"You children are supposed to be studying the multiplication facts and I find you playing games. I can't believe it. Now, I'm going to give you another fast fact test on Monday and if you don't pass that one, I might have to send you down to the principal's office."

Molly was scared. So was Juan. When Miss Bees left the room to go and get the rest of the class, Molly told the others how frightened she was.

" I'm scared. I don't know what happened when you get sent to the principal, but I know that it is bad." Molly whined.

Juan surprised the two girls when he said, " I am not afraid of the principal, but I am worried that Miss Bees heard me speaking English when we were playing the game."

That reminded Molly that she hadn't told Sue about Juan and the big black car. Now that would have to wait until Monday.

CHAPTER 17:   CARNIVAL PROBLEMS

Over the weekend, Molly and her family had a few chances to play the card game that Mr. Plies had taught them. They played it with the flash cards and they played it with a pack of playing cards. Her parents were impressed at how quickly Molly could multiply numbers times **10**. She told them about how Juan had figured out the pattern.

But they didn't get to practice as much as Molly would have wanted. Her father had to spend some time on work he had brought home from his office. Her mother had to make lots of calls finalizing the details for the carnival. The long awaited carnival was only a week away. On Saturday night, Mrs. Plies received some very upsetting news. Mrs. Gannett, one of the most popular vendors at the carnival, called to cancel her booth. The woman explained that her husband had become very ill and therefore she would not be able to bring her handiwork to sell at the carnival. Mrs. Plies told her that she hoped the Mr. Gannett would feel better.

Mrs. Plies joined her husband and daughter in the family room where they were watching some television after completing their last game of "War." She told them the bad news that Mrs. Gannet would not be coming to the carnival. When her husband asked her if that meant the parents' organization would earn less money, Mrs. Plies explained that they would only lose the fifty dollars that the vendors had to pay for the booth. However, many people came to the fair just to see what Mrs. Gannett would bring that year. Mrs. Gannett sewed beautiful handmade clothes. She also made charming dresses for dolls that were also very popular.

"Does she make beautiful dresses like the ones that Sue wears?" Molly asked her mother.

"No, Molly, but that gives me an idea. Maybe Mrs. Tract would like to have a booth." Molly's mother answered.

"But, Mom, she probably doesn't have lots of dresses already made. Sue wears the same ones over and over." Molly explained to her mother.

Mr. Plies joined the conversation. "She wouldn't have to have lots of dresses already made. She could just have a few samples and then take orders for dresses she could make later."

"But, Dad," Molly told him. "Sue said that Mrs. Tract doesn't even get off the couch much. She's sick or something."

"She looked all right that day we went to see Miss Bees," her father said.

"I'll call her tomorrow," Mrs. Plies chipped in. And she did.

On Sunday afternoon, Mrs. Plies didn't ask Mrs. Tract if she wanted to have a booth at the carnival. Instead she called and asked if she could come over to see her. Mrs. Tract tried to say no, but when Mrs. Plies wanted to do something, it was very difficult to stop her. She asked Molly if she wanted to go with her to see Sue.

"Sure!" Molly answered enthusiastically. She wanted to see Sue, but even more she wanted to see if her mother could convince Mrs. Tract to have a booth at the carnival. They arrived at the Tract house at about 1:00 p.m.

After saying hello to Mrs. Tract, Molly went upstairs with Sue. When Molly told Sue what her mother was going to do, Sue was thrilled. She thought it was a great idea. The two girls decided to creep down the stairs to listen to their mothers talk.

They had trouble hearing everything the women were saying, but they did hear Mrs. Tract try to refuse to have a booth. But then Mrs. Plies began speaking again.

"Your work is so beautiful," she told Mrs. Tract. "I would love to buy a dress for Molly and I am sure my friends would love to buy dresses for their daughters. I would also love to buy one for my sister's little girl. She's just two years old. I love the look of smocked dresses on toddlers."

Mrs. Tract surprised her guest by saying that she had some dresses already made for little girls aged two or three. She explained that she had made them for the sister that she hoped Sue would have one day. Then she told Mrs. Plies that she had even made some dolls dresses that matched those dresses.

Mrs. Plies was overjoyed. She knew what a big seller those doll dresses would be. She explained to Mrs. Tract the plan her husband had suggested. Mrs. Plies could bring her finished dresses to the carnival. Then, she could take orders for other dresses.

For a moment, Mrs. Tract looked excited. However, a moment later she retreated into the cushions on her couch. "I just can't do it," she told Mrs. Plies. "It's too much work. I don't even know if I can find the dresses I made. It was so long ago. Now there is such a mess here."

"How about if I help you?" Mrs. Plies asked.

Coming out of her hiding spot in the stairway, Sue said, "I could help too."

"And so could I," added Molly. "When can we start?"

"How about right now?" Mrs. Plies asked. "Let me just call my husband and tell him that we won't be home this afternoon. And then we will start the hunt to find the missing dresses. While we're at it, we can straighten up some. And we can find a place for you to do your sewing. And we can figure out how much you should charge for your dresses. And we can think about how to decorate your booth. Oh, the booth. Well, Mr. Plies and I will pay your booth fee."

"Whew, slow down please, Mrs. Plies," said Mrs. Tract. "You're going too fast for me. And I can pay the booth fee myself, but thanks for offering."

Molly giggled at what Mrs. Tract was saying. She was used to seeing what her mother was like when she started a new project. Sue was smiling too. She was smiling because her mother was smiling.

The two women and the two girls started the hunt for the dresses. Mrs. Tract found two little girl dresses with doll dresses that matched them in a box under her bed. She told the others that she knew she had made more, but couldn't remember where they were. Mrs. Plies suggested that they start in the living room and work out from there.

Molly knew what her mother was doing. Her mother just wanted to get all of the clutter out of the room. It didn't take Mrs. Plies long to get the situation organized. They made three piles. There was one pile of things to be thrown out, one pile of things to be put away, and one pile of things for Mrs. Tract to look at later to decide if they should be kept or trashed. The young girls bagged up the trash and took it out to the garbage cans in the garage. When the trash was gone, the room looked much better. While Mrs. Tract was busy putting away the items that she was keeping, Mrs. Plies and the girls went on to the dining room.

It would have been a beautiful room, if it wasn't filled with litter. It looked as if Mrs. Tract just dumped the mail on the table every time it came. When she joined them in the room, she explained to Mrs. Plies that was exactly what she had done. She told her that when the mail came, she took out the bills and dumped everything else on the dining room. She had been doing that ever since Sue's father had left two years before.

Molly couldn't believe how high the pile was. However, she could believe how anxious her mother was to organize the stack. After asking Mrs. Tract for some more garbage bags, she put Molly and Sue in charge of picking out all of the advertisements and flyers that had come in the mail. The girls were very good at finding the colorful booklets and throwing them into the garbage. In the meantime, Mrs. Tract and Mrs. Plies went through the other letters. Once again, they made the three piles. After opening the envelopes and scanning the contents, they decided whether that mail should go in the keep-pile, the throw away-pile, or the think about-pile.

"How's this going to help my mother find the missing smocked dresses?" Sue whispered to Molly.

"It's not," Molly whispered back. "But my mother can't work in anyplace that's not orderly. I think she's trying to show your mother how to clean up the clutter. Do you have any idea where the dresses might be?"

"I bet they're in the sewing room upstairs. When we finish in the dining room, I'll suggest that next."

But before Sue could make that suggestion, Molly's mother made a discovery. She found a letter addressed to Sue. In fact, she found about ten letters addressed to Sue. She was going to give them right to the little girl, but stopped and handed them to her mother. Mrs. Tract looked at them and turned to Mrs. Plies.

"I never saw these. I mean, I must have seen the enveloped when I threw them on this table, but I never paid any attention to what they were, who they were to, or who they were from. They're from Sue's father. I wonder what he wrote to her."

"Perhaps you should find the first one and open it." Mrs. Plies responded. Then she put the letters in order based on the postmarked dates and handed the first one to Mrs. Tract. After opening it and quickly reading its contents, Mrs. Tract put it down and went to get a tissue. When she returned, she gave the letter to Sue.

Sue couldn't believe that she had received mail. She couldn't remember ever getting any letters that were addressed just to her. She began to read,

"*Dear Susie,*

I miss you very much. I want you to know how much I love you."

Sue looked at her mother. "Who is this from?" she wanted to know.

"It's from you father. I'm so sorry Susie. I didn't even know he had sent them. We'll go through all of them tonight. I'll even help you write an answer."

Molly's mother suggested that they could go through the letters right then. She and Molly would go home. If it was all right with Mrs. Tract, she would come back the next morning and they would continue the hunt for the missing smocked dresses. At that time, they would decide how much to charge for the dresses, how to decorate the booth, and what the order forms should look like. Molly took her mother's hand and led her to the door. When she looked back she saw that Sue and her mother were busy reading the letters. They didn't even hear

the Plies leave.

CHAPTER 18: ANOTHER TEST

Molly couldn't wait to see Sue the next day at school. She was amazed when Sue entered the classroom. The little girl who was usually so sad was now all smiles. She went right over to Molly's desk to thank her for bringing her mother to her house. She told her that she and her mother read all the letters her father had sent her. Each of the letters explained how much her father loved and missed her and how much he wanted to see her. Her mother had helped her write a letter back to him.

Sue told Molly, "I told my father all about how you and your mother came and helped Mom and me clean up our house. And I told him how much I was looking forward to seeing him."

Before Molly could respond, Miss Bees hollered at the class to take their seats so that she could hand out the morning worksheets. Molly was so busy working on her papers in the morning that she forgot all about the fast fact test that they would have to take at recess time.

At lunchtime, she sat with Sue and Juan and they reviewed all of their tricks and all of the Stinky Finkys. Juan wondered how many of their classmates were working on schoolwork during lunch. The three students figured out they would be fine unless one or both of the unsolved Stinky Finkys were on the test.

When recess time came and Miss Bees told them to turn over their papers and begin Molly wasn't surprised to see that Miss Bees had put both of those facts on the test. There they were: **6 x 7** and **8 x 8**. She thought about just putting down her pencil, but then she changed her mind. This time, she decided, she would do as many of the facts as she could.

5 x 6 = 30 She knew that from the clock: half past the hour.

4 x 7 = 28 Double, Double. **7+7 is 14. 14 +14 is 28.**

1 x 3 = 3 One is the Mirror

0 x 8 = 0 Zero is the hero

9 x 4 = 36 She quickly did Juan's finger trick to do that one.

2 x 6 = 12 The double fact about the dozen eggs.

3 x 4 = 12 She remembered that from the first day Juan showed them the fact on the board. Just to double check she doubled **4** and got **8** and then counted on four more: **9, 10, 11, 12**

1 x 7 = 7 Mirror again

6 x 6 = 36 Juan's missing number trick: **6 X 6 = ___ 6.**

0 x 4 = 0 Zero is the hero again

7 x 9 = 63   Finger trick

7 x 7 = 49 Lucky 7s. (She wondered what Miss Bees would think if she wrote 49ers on her paper.)

5 x 2 = 10 Turn around Doubles: **5+5** is **10**, Shall we start again.

1 x 6 = 6 Mirror

7 x 6   There it was. She hoped Sue wouldn't cry when she saw it. It was the **6** and the **7** fact with the numbers Sue hated. But she just skipped it and went on.

8 x 1 = 8 Turn around Mirror

5 x 7 = 35 Turn around and count by 5

6 x 8 = 48 Dad's Stinky Finky. As she wrote the number she whispered, "I know the answer I am great."

9 x 2 = 18 Turn around Doubles about two baseball teams

2 x 9 = 18 Hey, it was just the turn around fact of the one right next to it.

4 x 0 = 0 Zero is the hero

3 x 3 = 9 Doubles plus one set ,**3 + 3 = 6** then count on **3** more: **7,8, 9**

8 X 9 = 72 Turn around Nueve Finger trick

5 x 1 = 5 Turn around Mirror

2 x 7= 14 Doubles. She pictured the two weeks on the calendar.

9 x 3 = 27 Finger trick

8 x 8 She skipped that one.

7 x 8 = 56 The number line. What comes before 7 and 8? 5 and 6

4 x 5 = 20 Count by 5s

4 x 9 = 36 Finger trick. It was faster than the Double, double.

0 x 9 = 0 Zero is the hero

Molly couldn't believe that Miss Bees had not yelled at them to stop yet. She had time to go back to the two facts she skipped. She looked at **7 x 6**. Maybe she could figure it out. She thought about what she did know. She did know that **6 X 6** was **36** because of Juan's Stinky Finky. So **7 X 6** would be another group of **6**. She started to count on **6** more when Miss Bees screamed "Pencils up."

Miss Bees scurried around the room picking up the papers. As she looked at the papers, she got an unattractive smirk on her face.

"None of you have passed," she sneered. "I guess we will have to see what the principal thinks about your failures. Maybe Mr. Spencer will forbid you from going to the carnival. Instead of playing games, maybe you should have been studying."

Molly started to tell Miss Bees that they were playing a game to help them study, but once again decided that it would be better to be quiet. She also decided that this time she would tell her parents right away that she hadn't passed the fast fact test. If only they could have come up with a Stinky Finky for **6 x 7** and one for **8 x 8**. When Miss Bees went to get the rest of the class from recess, Molly had time to ask Juan and Sue to meet her after school. She checked to see if Sue were crying

and was pleased to see that she wasn't.

CHAPTER 19: FIFTH STINKY FINKY

Molly did all of her afternoon worksheets and filed them in the correct baskets. When it was time for the walkers to leave the classroom, she got up with Sue and Juan and left the room.

"I can't believe that Miss Bees might send us to Mr. Spencer. Do you think he will forbid us from going to the carnival?" Molly asked the others as the walked to the cafeteria.

"I don't think so, but we can ask your mother. What do you think Juan?" Sue wanted to know.

"I don't want to go to the principal. I don't really care about going to the carnival, but the principal might look at my records. Then everyone will find—oh, never mind."

"But Mr. Spencer probably doesn't speak Spanish so he can't read your records," Molly said trying to make Juan feel better.

"They aren't really in Spanish. Miss Bees never checked them," Juan answered just as they reached the cafeteria. "Hey, where are your mother and the other ladies?"

Molly didn't know. She also didn't know how she would get home now that she had missed the bus. When she told the others her new problem, Juan had a solution.

"You can use my cell phone to call your mother and ask her to come and pick you up," he suggested.

"Do you have a cell phone?" Molly asked. "Is that how the guy in the car knows where to pick you up?"

"What car?" asked Sue.

"I forgot to tell you about the car," Molly answered. "My mother and I saw Juan get into a great big black car the other day. Is the car part of the secret?"

Juan explained that it was. He promised the girls that he would be able to tell them his whole story in a few days. Then he gave Molly his cell phone. She called her mother, but there was no answer. Now what would she do, she wondered.

Sue suggested that they go to her house. Molly called her

mother again and left her mother a message that she was going to Sue's house. Sue asked Juan if he would like to come too. He told the girls that he thought he should go home, but that he would try to think of something to say to Mr. Spencer if they were sent to his office the next day. The girls said they would also try and figure out what they would say to Mr. Spencer. While Juan was walking away, they saw him open his phone to make a call.

Molly was very surprised when they arrived at Sue's house and saw that her mother's car was in the driveway. She was even more amazed when they went into the house and saw that it looked perfect. When her mother greeted the children, she explained that Mrs. Tract and she had worked all day cleaning and organizing. Both women were excited to show them that they had found the missing dresses. Mrs. Plies explained that they had set up Mrs. Tract's sewing room and that Sue's mom thought she could finish a few more dolls' dresses before the carnival. They were working on the order form. Once they designed it, Mr. Plies could type it on his computer and print out copies. Then all they had to do was figure out how to decorate the booth.

"We could help make the decorations," Sue suggested. "It would be fun."

"But we won't be able to see how it looks at the carnival. Miss Bees won't let us go," Molly murmured.

"What was that?" Mrs. Plies asked.

Molly explained what had happened that day when they retook the fast fact test. She told her mother that both of the still unknown Stinky Finky facts were on the test. In fact, all of the Stinky Finkys were on it. She next told them, "Miss Bee's is going to send us to the principal and he is going to forbid us from going to the carnival."

Mrs. Plies was not happy. She said, "Don't worry Molly. Your father and I will ask for another meeting with Miss Bees and with Mr. Spencer too. And we will work harder to figure out a Stinky Finky for those last two facts."

"A what? What are Stinky Finkys?" Mrs. Tract wanted to know.

Molly and Sue took turned explaining what they were. Mrs. Tract thought they were great. She said that she wished someone had shown her a trick like that when she was in school. Then she asked which were the two facts that were left. Sue told her it was **6 x 7** and **8 x 8**.

"Oh my. **6** and **7**. Do you remember that your father always used to say that our house was 'at sixes and sevens?'" Mrs. Tract asked her daughter.

"I always thought it had something to do with the fact that I was only seven," Sue said. "I thought it was why he left us."

"No, no, Susie," Mrs. Tract said while giving her daughter a hug. "Being 'at 6s and 7s,' means being all confused or disorderly. Like our house was before Molly's mother helped me. But fortunately, it's better now." Mrs. Tract stopped and looked up at the ceiling. The others wondered what was the matter.

"Listen to that again," she said. "Our house was at sixes and sevens, but fortunately it isn't any more. That's a Stinky Finky."

"But I don't get it," Sue told her mother.

"**6 x 7** is **42**. The forty-two is in the sentence. It's just hidden like a secret clue. Listen as I say *"fortunately,"* doesn't that sound like *Four Two net lee*. Four two is forty-two. All you have to do is remember our house before and our house now and you'll remember the answer."

"That's a great one, Mrs. Tract." Molly said. "We could just write that sentence on the back of our Stinky Finky cards. Then we could put a little **4** over the first part of *fortunately* and a little **2** over the middle of it. I love it! Now we only have one left. "

Mrs. Plies was the one who realized how late it was and said that it was time to go home. Mrs. Tract agreed to come to the Carnival Committee meeting the next day after school. She also said that if there were a meeting with Miss Bees, she wanted to go to that, too.

Molly was anxious to get home to show her father the new Stinky Finky. Her mother was anxious to put that new Stinky Finky on their chart. She was also anxious to show him the order form for Mrs. Tract's dresses. She was sure that he could figure out how to print it.

Molly became very sullen at dinner that night. Mrs. Plies had already explained to her husband about the threat that Miss Bees had made to the three children that day. He tried to cheer up his daughter by explaining that he didn't think Miss Bees could prevent the children from attending the carnival and that he and her mother would go with her to see the principal if necessary. He suggested that they play a game of War after dinner was done and the dishes were put into the dishwasher.

While they were playing the game, Molly's spirits improved. She discovered that she was able to quickly give the answers to many of the facts. Her mother explained to her that was happening because she was practicing. Her mother continued to say that the more practice she did, the easier this mathematical skill would become.

Molly agreed. "If the practice is as much fun as this game, I don't mind doing it."

When the game was over, Molly went upstairs to write her spelling words. She heard the phone ring, but continued writing the words. When her homework was completed, she packed up her book bag and got ready for bed.

She expected that both of her parents would come upstairs to read books with her, but only her father arrived. He explained that her mother had received one more disappointing call. Another one of the ladies who had always baked cookies for the carnival called to cancel. Her husband had come down with the same flu as Mrs. Gannett's husband. Now Mrs. Tract was making lots of calls to see if she could find another mother who could make cookies for the carnival.

Mr. Plies found the page that they were on in the book that they were reading and sat down next to Molly's bed to begin reading.

Before he could start, Molly asked him a question. "Dad, I've been thinking about Miss Bees and going to the principal and missing the carnival."

"I know you have, pumpkin," he replied. "But you don't have to worry about missing the carnival."

"I hope so Dad," Molly continued. "But I've been thinking that if Miss Bees sends us to the principal we could tell him how she's been leaving us alone in the classroom. And how Juan saw her smoking. That would get her in big trouble."

"But would that help you?" her father asked. "I know that you are very angry at Miss Bees, but getting her into trouble with the principal will just make her madder at you. Right now she's only angry because you don't know your facts, but if you do something to get her into trouble, she'll only get angrier. And remember, Molly, you have to stay in her class until June. Isn't there another way you could deal with her? Your mother told me that you almost completed the fast fact test this time. That's a great improvement. Maybe you could explain that to Miss Bees. Maybe she would give you another chance. How many facts did you miss?"

Molly explained that she had only missed the two Stinky Finkys

6 x 7 and **8 x 8.** She also told him the Sue's mother had come up with a

Stinky Finky for **6 x 7** and told him the story about how their house

used to be 'at sixes and sevens, but fortunately it was all clean now'."

Mr. Plies loved that Stinky Finky.

"So the only one left is **8 x 8 = 64.** Think of how many facts you

have already learned. Now there is only that one left." After kissing his

daughter goodnight, Mr. Plies went down stairs to see if his wife had

found someone to bake for the carnival. Molly fell asleep repeating **8 x**

8 = 64 over and over.

6 x 7

Secret Code

6   x   **7**

Our house was all at sixes and sevens

=   4   2

But   fortunately we cleaned it up.

CHAPTER 20: SIXTH STINKY FINKY

On the bus to school Tuesday morning, Molly told Addy, "Miss Bees is threatening to send Juan, Sue, and me to the principal . But my father also told me not to be angry."

Addy thought that was good advice. "Maybe if you asked nicely, Miss Bees will give you another chance."

Molly wasn't sure. She knew that Miss Bees would give Addy another chance because Addy was the top student in the class. But Addy never needed another chance because Addy always got everything right the first time she tried.

Molly also told Addy all about the booth that Mrs. Tract was going to have at the carnival. Addy was very excited that Mrs. Tract was going to sell dolls' clothes. Addy even offered to help make the decorations for the booth when Molly told her that Sue and she were going to make them for Mrs. Tract. Both girls thought that maybe some of their other friends would help too.

"I sure hope that I will be able to go to the carnival," Molly moaned.

"Me, too," Addy agreed.

Molly didn't have a chance to talk to Sue or Juan until lunchtime. She had lots of things to discuss with them. First, she had to make sure that Sue was going to stay after school to make decorations for her mother's booth. When Juan heard about that, he offered to stay with them and help. Then she had to tell them about her conversation with her father the night before. Both of the other children agreed that making Miss Bees angrier would hurt them in the long run. Juan was especially relieved because he didn't want Miss Bees to know that he had seen her smoking. He explained that he had seen her when he was going to get into his car to go home after school. He didn't want Miss Bees to know about his black car.

Then Sue interrupted Molly because they hadn't told Juan about the new Stinky Finky for **6 x 7**. He really liked the idea of a secret message being hidden in the sentence about Sue's house.

Molly just had time to inform her recess detention mates about the lady who wouldn't be baking for the carnival when lunchtime was over and they had to go back to their classroom.

Molly tried to concentrate on the worksheets that Miss Bees handed out after lunch. Miss Bees hadn't said anything to them about sending them to the principal yet, but Molly thought that maybe she was just waiting until recess. She was almost positive that Miss Bees would make sure that everyone in their class knew that they had to go see Mr. Spencer.

But that didn't happen. Miss Bees just told Sue, Juan, and Molly to stay in the room when she took their classmates out to recess. The teacher left with the rest of the class.

"Do you think she forgot?" asked Sue.

"Maybe she's going to come back and get us," Molly answered. They all looked nervously at the clock.

Juan was the one who finally spoke. "I've been thinking about that lady who can't bake cookies for your carnival," he said quietly. "I've been thinking that maybe my mamagrande could help."

"Could she make those delicious Mexican Wedding cookies?" Sue wanted to know.

Molly joined in remembering how delicious those cookies were.

She told Juan that she could have eaten hundreds of them.

"I know what you mean," Juan said. "One time my parents told me that I could eat as many as I wanted. I ate them and ate them, but then I was sick for days. Now I only eat a few at a time, but they..."

Molly stopped him. "Say that sentence again," she commanded.

"What sentence?" Juan wanted to know.

"The one about when you ate and ate," Molly told him.

So Juan repeated the sentence. "I ate and I ate and I was sick for days."

Molly jumped up and danced around her desk. "That's it," she exclaimed. "That's the last Stinky Finky. It's the one for **8 X 8**."

Then she slowly explained it to Sue and Juan. "I <u>ate</u>. The word for putting food in your mouth and chewing it up sounds just like the number eight. So I ate and I ate would be the **8 X 8**. Then Juan said he was 'sick for days.' Doesn't 'sick for' sound like six four and six four turns into sixty-four. My dad told me that fact last night. It's a Stinky Finky like the one Sue's mother made up. It's another secret code in a sentence.

"It's a great Stinky Finky!" Sue said excitedly.

The three children were chanting, "I ate and I ate and I was sick for days," when the door opened and Miss Bees entered.

"What is all that racket?" she demanded to know.

Now we are in really big trouble, Molly thought. Miss Bees would surely send them to Mr. Spencer at once. There would be no carnival for them this year.

Her depressing thoughts were interrupted by Sue's voice. "We were so loud, Miss Bees," Sue said calmly. "because we just came up with a way to remember the last fact that we were having trouble with. It was **8 x8** "

"I noticed that you all got that one wrong on your fast fact test. You all missed **6 x 7** too."

Molly nervously entered the conversation. "But they were the only ones we missed, Miss Bees. We're getting much better at multiplication. Do you think that we could have one more try before you send us to Mr. Spencer and we have to miss the carnival?" she asked her teacher.

Miss Bees studied the three children. "You are ruining my record. All of my students always master multiplication. I am so disappointed in you three. But I will give you one <u>last</u> chance."

Molly, Sue, and Juan could not believe it.

Miss Bees continued, "I can't give you the quiz on Wednesday because I have to go to a meeting at recess time but that I will give you the retake of the fast fact test on Thursday."

"We'll get the all right then," Sue told her.

"We really will," Molly added.

"Si, si," Juan added.

8 x 8

CODED MESSAGE

8   x   8   =   6   4

I ate and I ate, and I was sick for days.

CHAPTER 21: MORE CARNIVAL WOES

Molly couldn't wait to get to the cafeteria. She wanted to tell her mother that Miss Bees was going to let them take a retest. She also wanted to tell her about the final Stinky Finky. When the three children entered the room, they found Molly's mother introducing Sue's mother to the other ladies who were helping organize the carnival that year. Mrs. Tract had brought a couple of her dresses to show the other committee members. Everyone agreed that the dresses would be a big seller at the fair.

"Will we have time to decorate her booth?" Mrs. Bonney wanted to know.

"Mrs. Gannet always brought her own decorations," Mrs. Bettcher explained.

"It won't be a problem," Molly's mother explained. "Mrs. Tract has her own helpers to make her decorations." Then she pointed to Molly,

Sue, and Juan.

The two mothers walked over to their daughters and Juan. Both had large bags filled with art supplies. Mrs. Tract quickly explained that she and Mrs. Plies had gone shopping and bought all of the things the children would need to make the decorations for the booth. She then produced two cardboard patterns for them to trace on the colored poster paper she had purchased. They were both outlines of girls' dresses: one was small and one was large. She told the children that all they had to do was to trace the patterns and cut out the dresses. Then she would show them how to finish the decorating tomorrow.

"We can do more tonight," Sue told her mother.

"Not tonight, sweetheart," her mother answered. "Tonight we have something else we to do."

"What?" inquired Sue.

"It's a surprise. You'll just have to wait and see," Mrs. Tract replied mysteriously.

"Speaking of surprises," Molly interjected. "We had a great surprise today. Miss Bees is going to let us take the fast fact test again.

And Juan figured out a Stinky Finky for **8 x 8**. It's about his grandmother's cookies—oh, Mom, his grandmother could make cookies for the carnival—the Stinky Finky is ' I ate and I ate and I was sick for days.' Get it, 'sick for' sounds like six four which turns into sixty-four." Molly stopped to take a breath.

"Slow down, Molly," her mother suggested. "What did you say about Juan's grandmother?"

"She makes cookies. They're great. And Juan said she could make them for the carnival."

"Juan said?" her mother questioned.

Realizing the Molly had almost given away Juan's secret that he could speak English, Sue quickly suggested that Juan could write his phone number on a piece of paper and Mrs. Tract could call his grandmother that night and make arrangements for the cookies and the carnival. Mrs. Tract thought that was a good idea and the two mothers returned to the table where the other committee members were working.

"Nice job, Sue," Juan whispered. "Molly almost gave me away. But after tomorrow I will probably be able to tell you the whole story anyway. Either that or I will be moving again. I hope not. I like it here!."

"I hope you can stay," Molly said. "Sorry about almost giving away the secret."

"I hope you can stay too," Sue added. "Now let's look at the stuff my mom wants. I wonder how many we're supposed to make. I guess we should just keep working until we run out of paper."

"How many will that be?" Molly wanted to know.

"Let's see if we can figure it out." Juan said. Holding the big pattern up to the poster paper, he calculated that they could make three big dresses out of each piece. Then Molly did the same thing with the small pattern. They figured out that they could make five small dresses from each sheet. Then they counted the number of sheets of poster paper. Mrs. Tract had given them **18** sheets of colorful poster paper.

"Let's put the paper in two piles. How many should we put in each pile?" Molly wanted to know.

"Nine," answered Juan.

"How did you figure that out?" Molly asked.

"I thought about when I first showed you about equal groups. Remember when I first drew those pictures on the board of the circles with the squares in them. I pictured two circles and thought about how many squares would go into each so that we would have 18 squares altogether. Two groups of what would be **18**. That's nine, cause nine plus nine is eighteen."

"That makes two baseball teams," Sue chimed in.

At the mention of baseball, Juan got a funny look on his face. He quickly recovered and counted out nine sheets of paper for one pile and nine for the other. "I'll start tracing the big pattern," he informed them. "That will give your mother **27** big dresses to decorate her booth."

Sue smiled. "You figured that out by multiplying **3 x 9**, didn't you? And you didn't even look at your fingers for the finger trick."

"I know," replied Juan. "I'm starting to just remember the answers."

"I am, too," Molly said. "My mom said it's because I'm practicing and practicing."

"Me, too," Sue said agreeing with the others.

"I can figure out how many small paper dresses we'll make," Molly commented. "If we can make **5** dresses from each sheet and we have **9** sheets, that would be, hmm?" Molly looked down at her hands and quickly did Juan's finger trick. "That would be **45** dresses. I can remember the answer to lots of facts but I like to have the tricks to use if I forget one."

"Hey, look at us." Sue said happily. "We're multiplying. I never thought I would ever use that math! I didn't know why we needed to do it."

"Me either," Molly and Juan said at the same time.

While Juan traced the big pattern, Sue traced the small one. Molly cut out the dresses from the poster paper. They quickly produced the dresses. Before they knew it, it was time to clean up. Mrs. Tract thanked them for making the dresses. She told them that they would be drawing the smocking on the paper dresses tomorrow. After helping to clean up their paper scraps, she thanked them again. She told Sue to hurry, as they had to go find out what the surprise was.

CHAPTER 22: CARNIVAL CATASTROPHE

All of the Plies had good news to share when they sat down to dinner. Molly told her father that Miss Bees was going to let them take the fast fact test over again on Thursday. She thanked him for his good advice. Then she told her father about the new Stinky Finky for **8 X 8**. She knew her mother would be happy to be able to fill in the last numbers on the Stinky Finky chart. Mrs. Plies was delighted. She had other good news. She told her husband and daughter that her current problem was solved. She had called Juan's grandmother and asked her if she could bake cookies for the carnival. Juan's grandmother said that she would be delighted to help. Mrs. Plies did comment, though, that Juan's grandmother did not have any kind of Spanish accent. She wondered whether the grandmother was the mother of Juan's father or Juan's mother.

Mr. Plies was excited about the upcoming baseball season. He had heard on his car radio that his beloved Boston Red Sox baseball team had finally signed Sean Ide as their new pitcher. He exclaimed that Ide had been at spring training down in Florida with the team but the final details of his contract had not been worked out until the night before. He thought that with the addition of this fabulous pitcher, the Red Sox might have another chance at the World Series. Fortunately for Mr. Plies, his wife and his daughter were also baseball fans. They became excited about the new addition to their team. The shrill ringing of the phone interrupted their conversation about Boston's new lineup.

Mrs. Plies answered the phone. Molly and her father could tell by the look on her face when she returned to the dining room, that something awful had happened.

"I can't believe this is happening," Mrs. Plies murmured, "And just three days before the carnival. We'll never have time to find a replacement."

"A replacement for what?" her husband asked her.

"The bounce around. That was the owner of the bounce around company. He finally returned my phone call. He told me that they can't bring their blow up trampoline to our carnival because they lost their insurance. Now what am I going to do? We will lose all the money that we gave them for a down payment and we will lose all the money that we would have made at the carnival. The bounce around was the biggest attraction."

Molly had never seen her mother so upset. However, her father remained calm.

"You won't have to worry about the deposit. Remember my firm helped to write the contract you signed. If the bounce around company doesn't show up for your carnival, you'll get your deposit back. I'll make sure of that."

Mrs. Plies thanked her husband, but she did not look any happier. She excused herself from the rest of the family and went back into her office to call the other members of the committee to let them know the bad news.

Molly knew that it would not be a good time to suggest a family game. She told her father she needed to do her homework. She took her book bag upstairs to her room. Once she had finished her spelling homework, she decided that she would make the Stinky Finky cards for the two last Stinky Finkys. Because she had the time, she also decided to make the cards for Sue and Juan.

When she went back down stairs to get more 3" by 5" cards, she saw that her mother was still on the phone. Her father had gone into the den and was watching television. Molly peaked in to see what he was watching.

She wasn't surprised to see that he was watching a sports show. The big story of the night was about the new Boston pitcher. Just as she was about to go upstairs to make the Stinky Finky cards, they showed a picture of that new member of their team, Sean Ide. Molly looked carefully at his face. He looked very familiar. However, Molly knew she could not have seen him before because he had played for the Houston Astros. Boston didn't even play them. But he did look very familiar.

Molly retreated back upstairs. After making the new Stinky Finky cards, she took out her whole set and practiced the way her father had shown her. She made the two piles: winner's pile and "need to practice" pile. This time there were no cards in the need to practice pile. Then she took out the box of flashcards that her mother had given her. Again she practiced her facts with the two piles. Again there were no cards in the "need to practice" pile. Molly felt proud of herself.

When her parents came up to read with her, she could tell that her mother was still very upset. Molly tried to cheer her up by telling her how well she had done when she practice her multiplication facts that night. Her mother smiled, but that smile soon disappeared. After reading another chapter in their book, her parents kissed her good night and left her room. However, her father crept back into the room to tell her not to worry about the carnival. He was sure that they would find something to replace the bounce around.

CHAPTER 23: THE MYSTERIOUS JUAN

Molly's Wednesday did not start off well. Her mother was still worried about the carnival. Her bus ride to school was awful. As soon as she got onto the bus, kids started to yell at her.

"How could your mother mess up the carnival so much," they screamed.

"Stop yelling at Molly," Addy said, "It's not her fault the bounce around won't be at the carnival." That only made the others on the bus yell louder.

Molly wasn't surprised that the kids on her bus had already heard that there would be no bounce around at the carnival. After all, Chase was a small town. However, she was surprised that they were yelling at her.

By the time she arrived in her classroom, Molly was sure that the entire school knew that there would be no bounce around at the carnival. She was also sure that everyone in her class would hate her. The first person she saw when she walked into the door made her believe that even more. It was John.

John was the tallest boy in their class. He always won all of the races when they had field days. He always was the first person picked when they chose up teams in physical education class. He was the leader of the boys in the class.

"Hey, Molly," he screamed in her face, "I heard that your mother ruined our carnival."

"Hey, John, leave her alone!"

Molly turned to see who was taking her side and talking back to John. It was Juan.

Molly was not the only person to be surprised that Juan was standing up to John. Most of the other boys in the class had followed John over to greet Molly when she first entered the classroom. They were just as amazed as she was.

"Just who do you think you're talking to?" John asked Juan.

But before he could answer, someone else questioned Juan. It was Shane and he asked the question that everyone who had heard Juan wanted answered.

"Can you speak English, Juan?" Shane wanted to know.

"Yeah," muttered Juan.

"You mean you could speak English all the time. That's great. You really fooled Miss Bees." Shane said excitedly.

Just as Shane finished his sentence, Miss Bees entered the classroom and told everyone to take their seats. Molly didn't get a chance to thank Juan for coming to help her when John was yelling at her. Miss Bees was about to hand out the morning worksheets when Addy raised her hand. She told Miss Bees that she had a note to bring down to the office because she wasn't going to be taking the bus home that afternoon. Miss Bees told her that she should bring it down to the office. Before Addy could get up, other girls raised their hands. Sarah, Shannon, Kaleigh, Kiley, Kate and Ellie all had notes saying that they were not going to be taking the bus. They were all going to stay after school to help make the decorations for the carnival. Molly was relieved that her friends were still going to help.

Miss Bees told the girls to bring their notes to the office. Just after they left, the door opened. Molly was surprised again. The person walking into the room was Sue. At least Molly thought it was Sue. This girl looked like Sue, but she wasn't wearing a dress and she had a different hairstyle. Whoever this was looked great.

"I'm sorry I'm late," the mystery person said.

It was Sue. As she walked back to her desk, she winked at Molly and mouthed, "I've got so much to tell you."

They didn't get a chance to talk until lunchtime. Molly walked timidly into the cafeteria and began to walk back to the table where she and Sue and Juan had been sitting. But that table was crowded. Many of the girls in the class had come back to talk to Sue and to find out about her new clothes and her new look. Most of the boys in the class, except John, had come back to talk to Juan.

When Juan started to talk, the girls stopped chatting. Everyone wanted to know how Juan had fooled Miss Bees. He told them that he had learned some Spanish from the morning cartoon shows and in his former town. When he realized that Miss Bees wasn't going to check his records, he just pretended that he could only answer her in Spanish.

When Juan finished his story, the boys went back to talking among themselves. The big topic of conversation was that the Red Sox had signed Sean Ide.

The girls went back to discussing Sue's new outfit and where she had bought it. She told them that her mother had taken her to the mall and that they had bought a couple of pairs of jeans and tops to match. Then her mother had taken her to a hair salon. Both of the Tract women had gotten matching hairdos. Molly told her that she couldn't wait to see Mrs. Tract. Sue explained that her mother was coming to the carnival meeting that afternoon.

Lunchtime ended too quickly for Molly. She had enjoyed seeing her classmates making a fuss over Juan and Sue. It was also fun not to have to think about the carnival with no bounce around.

After completing another set of worksheets, Molly saw that it was time for recess. She was glad that she didn't have to go outside because she was sure that students from other classrooms would have joined John yelling at her. She was also glad to have time alone with Sue and Juan. After giving him the Stinky Finky cards she had made the night before, she thanked Juan for helping her in the morning. She asked him if he was upset that his secret was now out. He told her that he wasn't. He had found out last night that his family was going to stay in Chase so he guessed that he would have to "learn English" quickly any way. Then Molly turned to Sue. She just couldn't believe how great Sue looked. She gave Sue her new Stinky Finky cards and told Sue just how she felt. Sue told Molly that Molly and her mother were the reason that Mrs. Tract had taken her to the Mall the night before. Her mother was so much better and was so excited about the carnival. Plus, when Mrs. Tract had seen the outfits that Molly wore, she had finally realized that Sue shouldn't be going to school in dresses every day.

"But I love your dresses now," Molly told her.

"I love them too," Sue explained. "But I don't love wearing a dress on the days when we have gym."

The three children were laughing when Juan asked a question.

"What's the big deal about that bounce around?" he wanted to know.

Molly explained that it was the most popular attraction at the carnival. Although the parents liked all the arts and crafts booths, the kids mostly liked the food and the bounce around. Now that there was no bounce around, Molly thought that the crowd for the carnival would be much smaller and that would upset her mother. Sue tried to cheer her up but before she could, Miss Bees returned with their classmates.

"Are you ready for the fast fact test tomorrow?" Miss Bees asked them. "I certainly hope you are."

Molly had forgotten all about the fast fact test. She hoped they were ready, too.

There was quite a crowd of students who went to the cafeteria at the end of the day. Even some of the boys had gone to the office during the day to get permission to stay after school. Those boys didn't know exactly what was going to happen, but they wanted to be there when it did. When they entered the room, Molly showed them where to put their backpacks and jackets. Then she organized them at tables and went to retrieve the paper dresses that Sue, Juan, and she had made the day before.

She almost didn't recognize Mrs. Tract who was talking with the other mothers. Mrs. Tract looked lovely. The new hairstyle looked as good on her as it did on Sue. She did recognize the lady who was talking to her mother. It was Juan's mamagrande.

Juan's mamagrande spoke perfect English.   Her mother was correct. There was no sign of any Spanish accent. The elegant elderly lady was telling Molly's mother that she had been baking all day and that she would have three kinds of Mexican Wedding cookies to sell at the carnival. Mrs. Plies thanked her for coming and all her hard work.

Molly could tell that her mother was still upset about the missing bounce around, but she thought it was great that her mother continued to work on the carnival. Then she had a thought about the booth in which mamagrande would sell her cookies. She asked both ladies about how it would be decorated.

Mamagrande did not know that she had to make decorations for her booth. Mrs. Plies told her not to worry. Then she looked over at all of Molly's classmates who had come that afternoon.   She told mamagrande that she would ask the fourth graders if they could come again the next day. She would think of something that they could make for her booth.

Just as she finished reassuring the elderly lady, Juan joined them. When he heard what problem was, he offered a solution.

"How about those big Mexican flowers made out of tissue paper?" he asked.

Molly's mother did a double take. Molly whispered to her that she would explain Juan's sudden ability to speak English when they went home. Juan's mamagrande thought the tissue paper flowers would be perfect. She told Mrs. Plies that tomorrow she would bring the materials to make the colorful decorations.

While Juan was speaking to his mamagrande and Mrs. Plies, Mrs. Tract had joined the fourth graders. She passed out the paper dresses and boxes of markers. Then she showed the children how to draw Xs on the top of the dresses so that it would look as if the dresses were smocked. The fourth grade girls loved the coloring. The fourth grade boys were not as excited about the project, but they tried their best.

By the time that parents started to show up to pick up their children almost all of the dresses were decorated. Mrs. Tract's booth was going to look wonderful. Before his classmates left, Juan asked them if they could come again tomorrow to work on a different project. Shane wanted to know if they were going to have to play with paper doll clothes again, but Juan assured him that it would be different. Mrs.

Tract thanked all of the boys and girls who had come to help. Mrs. Plies thanked all of the mothers who had shown up. After everything was cleaned up, the Plies went home.

Dinnertime conversation at the Plies house still concerned the missing bounce around. Mr. Plies told his wife that he had located the owner of the company. He added that after he had talked to him, the man had agreed to return the parents' organization's money. Mrs. Plies looked a little relieved, but Molly could tell that she was still upset.

"So tomorrow's the big retest," Mr. Plies said to Molly.

Molly nodded yes.

"I guess we will have to practice a lot tonight then. We want you to get them all right. But even more important, we want you to have learned those facts. You'll need them for the rest of your life."

After cleaning up the table, Mrs. Plies went and got the flash cards so that the family could play "War" and her Stinky Finky chart. Molly thought it was great that her mother would practice with her. She knew how upset her mother was about the carnival.

"We need to add the last two Stinky Finky clues to our chart," Mrs.

Plies explained.

6 x 6 = 36	**The Missing Number**
6 x 7 = 42	**Secret Code**
6 x 8 = 48	**Poem**
7 x 7 = 49	**Lucky Sevens**
7 x 8 = 56	**Number line**
8 x 8 = 64	**Coded Message**

Molly thanked her mother for making the chart. Her father passed out the cards and the Plies began to play their game.

Molly had a great time playing the game. She was able to give the answer for every fact. All of the Plies would join in whenever they came to one of the Stinky Finky facts. They were having a wonderful time, when the phone rang. Mrs. Plies didn't want to answer the phone. Every call that week had brought bad news. Sensing that, Mr. Plies went into the kitchen to find out who was calling. He had a very strange look on his face when he returned.

"Who was it?" his wife wanted to know.

"It was Juan. I thought you told me that Molly's new classmate could only speak Spanish. He speaks perfect English. He asked if he and his Mama grandest could come over."

Molly corrected her father. "It's mamagrande. I meant to tell you about Juan tonight. He can speak English just fine."

"When did you find that out?" her parents wanted to know.

"I didn't really do it. Sue did. She noticed that he was following our conversation and could answer yes or no when we asked a question. If he couldn't speak English, he wouldn't have even known what the question was."

"That Sue's a smart one," Molly's father commented. Molly was about to tell him all about Sue's new look, but her father continued talking. "Anyway, the mysterious Juan just called and asked if he and his mamagrande could come speak with you and me."

"He wants to talk to just us," Molly said. "What about Mom?"

"No, pumpkin," Mr. Plies said correcting her. "He wants to talk to your mother and me. He said it was a kind of a secret, but it might help the carnival."

"But what about me?" Molly wanted to know. "I kept his other secret."

"I don't know what to say, pumpkin. We'll just have to wait to see what he tell us."

Molly wasn't good at waiting. She paced in her room when Juan and his mamagrande were talking to her parents in her mother's office. When they called her to come down and see Juan, she almost refused to go. She was angry that he wouldn't tell her the secret.

But when she saw how relieved her mother looked, she almost forgave Juan. Almost. Her father looked pretty happy, too. It was her father that asked Juan and his mamagrande if they would like to join the family in a game of Multiplication War. Mamagrande told them that Juan had showed her how to play the game and that she thought it had helped him to learn the facts. They played for about an hour.

Although Juan wanted to continue playing, Mamagrande said that they had to go home and he had to go to bed. After all, she told him, he needed to be well rested so that he would do well on the retest.

Molly thought her parents would tell her what was going on when they went up to her room to read her the next chapter of their book.

But, they didn't.

CHAPTER 24: LAST CHANCE

As soon as she got onto the bus on Thursday morning, Molly told Addy about Juan's visit the night before. Addy didn't have any guesses about what Juan might have told her parents, but she told Molly that she had gotten permission to stay after school again. Addy added that her parents thought it was a great idea for the students to help decorate the booths for the fair. They wondered why no one had thought of that before.

Morning work went quickly. Lunchtime went quickly too. Molly tried to talk to Juan about what he had said to her parents the night before, but Juan was busy talking to the boys, especially Shane. Even John finally came over and told Juan that he thought he was a great actor for fooling Miss Bees and all the other grownups in the school. Molly also tried to talk to Sue but the girls who had come to help the day before surrounded her. They all wanted to know about the dolls' dresses that her mother was bringing to the carnival. Molly was happy for Sue and Juan, but a bit jealous. It wasn't until the end of lunchtime that she remembered what was going to happen that afternoon. Maybe she would never find out what Juan's secret was. If she didn't pass the fast fact test she wouldn't be allowed to go to the carnival. She really wanted to go to the carnival. She wanted to know if people would buy Mrs. Tract's dresses and if they would buy mamagrande's cookies. But most of all, she wanted to know what Juan's secret was.

After lunch, Molly tried to concentrate on her papers. Too soon, Miss Bees was taking the class out to recess. When her classmates left, Molly turned around to Sue and Juan. She wished them good luck on the fast fact test. They wished her good luck as well.

Miss Bees entered the room and swiftly passed out the fast fact paper. From her position in the front of the room, she announced loudly "Ready, set, go."

Molly flipped her paper over. She scanned the sheet quickly and realized that Miss Bees had given them the same test as she had the week before. She started the paper. She raced through the first row. This time she didn't have to skip **7 X 6** when she got to it. She smiled as she thought that "fortunately" she knew that answer. She continued working. Many of the facts she knew right away. Then she got to **8 X 8**.

Writing **64**, she smiled as she went on. There were only four facts left.

She finished those too. She expected Miss Bees to yell "Pencils up." But

she didn't. Molly wasn't sure what she was supposed to do. She had

never finished a fast fact test before. Perhaps I should look at it again.

Her mother was always telling her to double check her homework.

It was a good thing that Molly double-checked her paper. Right in

the first row, she found a mistake. She had written **21** instead of **12** for

the answer to **4 X 3**. Molly erased the wrong answer and quickly wrote

12. She had just finished checking the last row when Miss Bees hollered

"Pencils up." Molly lifted up her pencil triumphantly. She felt great.

She had done it.

When Miss Bees buzzed around the room collecting Juan's and

Sue's papers, Molly was able to turn around. Sue was smiling. So was

Juan. She gave them a thumb up signal. They signaled back. Miss Bees

told them to wait quietly while she went to get the class.

Finally, Molly had a chance to talk to Juan. She asked him what he

had talked about with her parents. He told her that it had to do with his

father and he wasn't sure the idea was going to work yet. He asked her if she could please wait patiently until tomorrow and he would tell her everything. Then turning to Sue, he said that he would tell them both everything. But, he continued, he wasn't going to tell anyone else and asked if they could keep another secret.

Molly and Sue were laughing when the class returned. Juan was laughing with them.

There were even more fourth graders who stayed after school on Thursday. Molly and her mother got them all organized. Juan's mamagrande passed out red, orange, yellow, and lime green tissue paper to some of the children. She gave others pipe cleaners and showed both groups how to fold the paper and twist the pipe cleaner around the folds. Then she opened up the folded paper and produced a beautiful flower. The girls thought it was beautiful. The boys were not impressed.

Just as they were about to begin, Molly's father arrived. Molly was really surprised to see him. He never came home from work that early. He went directly over to Molly's mother and gave her a big kiss. Then he whispered something to her. He motioned to Juan and his mamagrande. When they joined him, he whispered something to them too. Now all four of them were smiling and high fiving each other. Mr. Plies then opened his briefcase and brought out a large stack of papers. He told Mrs. Plies what needed to be done.

Mrs. Plies came over to the tables where the fourth graders were working. She asked everyone to stop making the flowers. Then turning to the boys, she told them that she had a new project for them. Instead of making the flowers, she asked them if they could fold up the papers that Mr. Plies had brought. When folded into thirds, the paper turned into a flyer that announced that this year's carnival would have a special attraction. The special attraction was a secret special attraction, but the flyer suggested that people who attended the carnival might want to bring their cameras with them.

The boys were happy to stop making flowers. While they folded the papers, they made guesses about what the secret special attraction would be. Molly noticed that Juan wasn't making any guesses. She guessed that he knew what the secret was.

When all the papers were folded and enough tissue paper flowers were made to decorate a couple of booths, Juan's mamagrande had a surprise. She produced a large box of her Mexican Wedding cookies for the fourth grade helpers to share. Everyone was glad they had come that afternoon. They were the first kids to learn about the surprise and they had delicious cookies too.

Molly enjoyed her cookies. She had quite a few but not enough to ruin her appetite for supper. That was lucky, because when her parents discovered she was pretty sure she had passed the fast fact test, her father suggested that they go out for pizza.

When they returned from dinner, Mr. Plies asked Molly if she wanted to play their game. Mrs. Plies asked if she could play too. They were having such a good time playing the family game that Molly almost forgot about her homework. Luckily, she remembered. Now that Miss Bees was no longer angry at her about the multiplication facts, it would not be good to make her mad about an incomplete homework assignment.

When her homework was done, her parents came up for the nighttime reading session. When that was finished and her parents were tucking her into bed, her father told her how proud he was of her. Molly went to sleep smiling.

CHAPTER 25: THE CARNIVAL

Molly was amazed when she got on the bus to go to school. Everyone on the bus already knew about the carnival's special attraction. The big kids asked Molly what the surprise was, but she explained that she didn't know. She told them she <u>really</u> didn't know.

When the bus arrived at school, she received another surprise. Her father was in the hallway walking toward the office. He was carrying the flyers that the boys had folded the day before. He waved to Molly but signaled that she should go on along to her classroom. Molly couldn't believe that he wasn't at work.

When she entered her classroom, everyone was talking about the big secret. Some of the boys were pretending that they knew what it was. Molly knew that the only person who really knew the secret was Juan. And he wasn't saying anything.

Before she could speak to either Juan or Sue, Miss Bees told everyone to go to their seats and she passed out the morning work. It seemed to Molly that there were more papers than usual, but maybe it was just because she was anxious for Miss Bees to tell her if she had passed the fast fact test. Miss Bees didn't say anything to Sue or Juan or her.

Once again at lunch, most of the fourth graders had come to sit at the table that she had been sharing with Sue and Juan. She was happy that Sue and Juan now had lots of new friends, but she wished that they would all go away so Juan could tell his secret.

When they returned to the classroom after lunch, Miss Bees busily handed out even more worksheets. Molly did her best on them, but she was really spending a lot of time watching the clock.

Finally it was recess time.   Now Miss Bees would have to tell them if they had passed. Now Juan could tell them what his big secret was.

Miss Bees never did tell them they passed. Nor did she give them their papers back. She just announced that it was time for recess and that finally everyone in her class could go outside.

"That's it," Molly wondered. "No good job and no announcement to the whole class that Sue and Juan and she had passed the test. No nothing." But Molly stopped herself from thinking those bad thoughts about Miss Bees. Molly knew what she had done and so did Juan and so did Sue. She got up from her desk and joined her classmates in the line to go outside for recess.

Molly thought that she would have a chance to talk to Juan at recess. But she didn't. They had to stay on the blacktop part of the school's playground because parents were out in the field setting up the booths for the carnival. When Juan saw his mamagrande stapling the flowers onto her booth, he ran to ask the recess aide if he could go help her. When Sue saw her mother putting the "smocked" paper dresses on her booth, Sue asked if she could help too. Soon, most of the fourth graders were offering to help. Molly didn't know what to do until she saw that her mother was working on a booth too. And so was her father. Molly was astonished that he had taken the whole day off from work.

Molly's parents were putting the finishing touches on the special surprise booth. It was pretty plain compared to the other booths. Molly's mother had hung blue material along the back of the booth. Her father was sticking letters onto a large jar. He had attached "D O N

A T and I", when Molly joined him.

"Hi, pumpkin. I bet Miss Bees made a big fuss about the fact that you passed the test," he said.

Molly told him that she hadn't, but that was all right. The people she most cared about knew what she had done to pass the test. Then she gave her father a big hug. She asked him what he was doing. He was just about to tell her, but the recess aide rang the bell signaling the end of recess and Molly had to go inside.

Because there were no more projects for the fourth graders to do, everyone went home right after school. Molly had never had a chance to talk to Juan. Her mother was busy with all of her files for the carnival when she got home. Her father was still helping with the final construction of booths. It was just like old times. Molly went to her room by herself.

She wasn't there long when she heard her parents calling for her. Dinner was ready. She went downstairs and into the dining room. There on the table was a big cake with icing that said "Great Job, Molly." Passing tests was turning out to be fun. First, she got pizza and now a cake.

Even though her mother still had lots to do for the carnival, she was the one who suggested a family game. For a change, the Plies decided to play a spelling game that Molly's grandmother had sent her months before.

Knowing how busy her mother was, Molly volunteered to go to bed early. After story time and hugs, she climbed into her bed. Tomorrow would be the carnival, she thought at she drifted off to sleep.

Early on Saturday morning, Molly heard the garage door open and her family's car pull out. She looked at the clock and saw that it was only 6:30 in the morning. She wondered who was leaving and where they were going so early. Then she remembered that it was the day of the carnival. She figured out that it must be her mother going to make sure everything was ready.

Her father was in an especially good mood. He even offered to make her French toast, but Molly decided that she would only have cereal. She wanted to have lots of room left for all of the good food at the fair. After breakfast, Molly watched some television. She kept asking her father when they could go to the school. He told her that they weren't supposed to go until at least ten o'clock.

The morning seemed to take forever, but finally it was time to go to the carnival. Mr. Plies was just about ready to drive out of the garage when he told Molly to check her seatbelt. He had forgotten something and would be right back. He returned to the car carrying their camera. He told Molly that it would have been terrible if he had forgotten the camera when he was the one who had suggested that people might want to bring them.

Although the trip to the school seemed to take five times as long as normal, the Plies finally arrived. They were surprised to see that the parking lot of the school was already filled and that there were cars parked along the entire length of the road that went into the school. The fair wasn't supposed to open for another half hour.

As they were walking down the road toward the school, a big black car passed them. Molly recognized that car. She knew it was Juan's. Then she remembered that Juan's mamagrande had to get to her booth.

Soon, Molly and her father arrived at the edge of the school property. They saw Mrs. Plies standing with Mr. Spencer and some other grown-ups. Mr. Spencer had one of those bullhorn things for making announcements. They could see him turn it on and bring it up to his lips.

"Ladies and gentlemen and children of Chase Elementary School, I declare the School Carnival open." There was a round of applause.

The fairground looked wonderful. It seemed to Molly that the booths were decorated better than ever before. Molly wanted to go to see Sue's mother's booth, but her father said that he had to go to the end of the fairground first. He told her that her mother would take her to all of the booths after they finished his mission.

They walked between the rows of the booths all the way to the end. There was the booth for the special secret surprise. Standing in front of it were Sue and Juan.

"What's going on?" Molly asked.

"I don't know," Sue answered. "Juan came and got me from my mother's booth. He said that you and I would get to see the special surprise first."

Juan just smiled.

Molly looked over at the booth. It didn't look the same as it did yesterday. Instead of the plain wooden front, there were banners along both sides and across the top. There were Red Sox banners all over the booth. But there was a cloth covering the front.

Then the three children heard someone ask, "Is it time yet, Dave?"

"Yes it is Dad," Dave (also known as Juan) answered.

Molly's father took down the cloth that had covered the booth. The girls saw Juan walk toward the man who was now standing with Molly's father.

"Dad, I want you to meet my friends, Molly and Sue," he said.

Molly looked up at Juan's father. He was dressed in a Boston Red Sox shirt and she knew she had seen him some place before.

"Molly," she heard her father saying, "say hello to Mr. Ide."

"Mr. Sean Ide," Molly stuttered. "Sean Ide, like the pitcher for the Red Sox. Oh, I'm sorry. I guess I shouldn't be calling you Sean."

"That's OK, Molly," responded the famous ball player. Dave's been telling me how you helped him in school. I wanted to thank you."

Molly was speechless. She knew that Juan's name was really Dave. But she hadn't known that his father was the new pitcher who would be coming to play for Boston.

"Molly," her father said interrupting her thoughts. "You're going to be the first person to have her picture taken with Juan's father, I mean Dave's father. Then I'm going to put some money in this jar that says DONATION. Sean didn't want to take any money for coming to the carnival. However, Juan came up with the idea of the donation jar. The money will go to the parents' organization."

Molly wished that she had worn her Red Sox sweatshirt. She stepped into the booth and her father took the picture. Then he told Sue to have her picture taken. Finally, Dave asked if he would take a picture of all three of them with his father. Mr. Plies was happy to take that picture too.

Just as Mr. Plies finished taking the third photo, Mrs. Plies arrived. She nodded her head toward the crowd that had gathered by the booth. Mr. Plies yelled out that all of the people waiting should get into a line and that Sean would be glad to meet them all. The line was much longer than any line for the bounce around had ever been.

Mrs. Plies took Molly and her friends around the carnival. They were all delighted to see that Mrs. Tract had a long line of people waiting to fill out order forms for her dresses and dolls' clothes. Mamagrande also had a long line in front of her booth. As they were walking through the fairgrounds they overheard many people talking into cell phones. They could hear them telling their friends and relatives that Sean Ide was at the fair and would sign autographs and take pictures as long as you donated to the Chase Elementary School Parents' Organization. They could see more and more people coming into the carnival site.

After taking one tour of the fairgrounds, Mrs. Plies took the children to a picnic bench. She bought them each some soda and mamagrande's cookies. Then she told them to wait there while she double checked attendance with the other members of her committee.

Molly smiled when she heard her mother say "double check." She told her friends how she had found her mistake when she double-checked her fast fact quiz.

"So, Dave," Sue said. "Why didn't you want anyone to know who your father was? You must be so proud of him."

"Oh, I am," Dave replied. "But in my last school when we lived in Texas, no one was my friend unless they wanted to meet my father. Then they would get mad at me because I couldn't throw a baseball at 90 miles per hour. Plus, I didn't know if we were going to stay here because my father thought he might get traded. I didn't want to make friends and then have to leave them again."

"Can they trade people?" Sue wanted to know. "Do you mean like slaves?"

"No," Dave corrected her. "They do that to professional athletes. Because I didn't know if we were going to stay in Chase, I figured that I wouldn't even try to have friends. But then Sue stood up to Miss Bees for me. And she didn't even know who my father was."

"You know, Dave," Sue said quietly. "I'm not really sure I know who your father is now. What does he do?"

Dave laughed. "See, Molly," he said. "Sue is my friend just because of me."

"I am, too." Molly chimed in. "Remember I was your friend when we were the kids with no recess. Wasn't it great the way that we figured out how to do all those multiplication facts. We sure showed Miss Bees, didn't we?"

When she saw the looks on the Sue's and Juan's faces, Molly knew she had said something very wrong. She sensed that someone was standing behind her. When she turned, she saw Miss Bees.

"Well, look who's here," Miss Bees said. "I hope you are enjoying the carnival. You know you almost missed it. Then you wouldn't have been able to meet Sean Ide. I hear that he is here at the carnival. I'm going over to get my picture taken with him now."

Molly was about to tell her that Sean Ide was Dave's father, but she stopped. "I hope you enjoy the carnival, Miss Bees," Molly said sweetly.

"So do I," said Sue. Dave nodded indicating that he did too.

"I hope you have a good time today," said Miss Bees haughtily. "It may be your last good time for a long time. On Monday, we are going to start division."

When she walked away, Molly looked at Sue and Dave. "I'm not worried," she said. "We'll figure that out too. Let's go enjoy the carnival."

ABOUT THE AUTHOR

Valerie H. Wilson is a retired teacher who taught everything from nursery school to college history. Most of her career was spent as an elementary school math specialist and math coordinator. She is married to a former superintendent of schools. The Wilsons currently reside in New Hampshire and Florida. They have two sons who are also teachers and six granddaughters, who loved this story.

Made in United States
Orlando, FL
08 February 2022

14574315R10113